Death in

He

little

Wi

And

sound

fores

said:

"I know."

"Let's get the horses and ride as fast as we can."

"They'll hear us."

"The fog'll give us some cover."

She took her hand from mine and we set off, scrambling underneath the fallen trees, groping in the fog for our horses—which were easier to smell than to see—and then mounting them blindly.

We hadn't gotten ten feet when shouts and shots erupted in the gloom. But they weren't aiming. They were running along the top of the ravine, firing at will and at random, thinking that if they put enough bullets into the air a couple of them were bound to hit us.

And the hell of it was: they were right.

ED GORMAN

CAVALRY MAN

THE KILLING MACHINE

HarperTorch
An Imprint of HarperCollinsPublishers

This is a work of fiction. Names, characters, places, and incidents are products of the author's imagination or are used fictitiously and are not to be construed as real. Any resemblance to actual events, locales, organizations, or persons, living or dead, is entirely coincidental.

❦

HARPERTORCH
An Imprint of HarperCollinsPublishers
10 East 53rd Street
New York, New York 10022-5299

Copyright © 2005 by Ed Gorman
ISBN-13: 978-0-06-073484-8
ISBN-10: 0-06-073484-1

First HarperTorch paperback printing: September 2005

HarperCollins®, HarperTorch™, and ❦ ™ are trademarks of HarperCollins Publishers Inc.

Printed in the United States of America

Visit HarperTorch on the World Wide Web at www.harpercollins.com

10 9 8 7 6 5 4 3 2 1

FOR MIKE SHOHL

Acknowledgments

My great thanks to Linda Siebels,
for her help with the manuscript.

CAVALRY MAN

THE KILLING MACHINE

"I hope this has been worth waiting for," scoffed the stout man. "I still say it looks like just another Gatling gun."

And so it did, a yoke-mounted machine gun on a carriage of wood and brass. The tires were steel, spoked. Nothing new. The Gatling gun had been around since 1862. This was 1881.

Four somber men in dark, expensive traveling suits walked around the gun, giving it expert appraisal.

How many men would it kill? And how quickly?

Around the world, politicians, kings, monarchs, mercenary leaders, and despots of every description wanted to know.

Noah Ford watched this inspection through his field glasses. A tall man with a long, melancholy face, dressed in trail-dusty denim shirt and jeans, he sat his pinto on a foothill that overlooked the field where the machine gun was being demonstrated.

The mountains looked cool and austere in the distance, much more inviting than the sticky eighty-one degrees that had kept his clothes damp since waking early this morning. Somewhere it was written that Montana Territory wasn't supposed to get this hot and humid. Somewhere.

Ford watched as the blond man in the tan suit stepped forward, smiling, gesturing for his helpers to come over. The next few minutes resembled the final routine in a magic show.

The blond man and his helpers lifted the yoke of the mounted gun and moved the weapon out farther into the empty field. Then he began walking around the gun, gesturing to various parts of it as he spoke, much as a magician would to the box he was about to disappear into.

Even in pantomime, the blond man was impressive. He had the skills of a good stage actor, one who spoke with his body as much as he did with his mouth. While the men hadn't burst into applause, their faces had taken on expressions of lively interest.

The first thing the blond man wanted to show his guests was how easily the gun could be loaded. There were loading problems with several models of the Gatling. There was no problem with this one. He then gave each man one of the bullets he would be using. In the past few years Gatling had started chambering rimfire copper-cased cartridges for more reliable use. He pointed out the improvements he'd made with the copper casings for his own weapon. They were superior to those Gatling used. Or so he claimed.

The final part of the prefiring demonstration was the discussion of the barrels that revolved around the central shaft. Six in the Gatling. Ten in this one. And then a two-minute walk-through of the cam-operated bolts that controlled the bullets. No misfires here; no, sir.

Ford scanned the faces, tight. If they weren't smiling, the guests were at least nodding along with the things the blond man was saying. Nodding in agreement. Yes, the blond man was saying, even given the considerable number of improvements Gatling had made on its weaponry—especially after it was bought by Colt—it still suffered from a number of problems . . .

And then—

—the only part of the demonstration that really mattered. The part that proved—or disproved—all the claims the blond man had made for his own unique machine gun.

"My God!" one of the four men shouted above the furor of the hand-cranked gun exploding into action.

Where the Gatling fired 900 rounds a minute, this fired 1,400. Where the Gatling bores were troublesomely tapered, these were round. And where the Gatling had never measured up to its potential in terms of accuracy, this weapon was ripping into the center of each of the three bull's-eye-style targets the blond man had set up before the demonstration.

Noah Ford again put his field glasses to his eyes.
There was real joy on the countenances of the four
men. They seemed almost childlike in their enthusiasm for the extraordinary show they were watching.
Probably not even women and whiskey could excite
them to this degree. What they were observing was
power, the kind of power that could topple king-
doms, democracies, empires. You could always buy
whiskey; you could always buy pussy. You couldn't
always buy power.

The air was hazy blue with drifting gunsmoke;
the mountains boomed with the echoes of the relentless gunfire. And then, in the ensuing aftermath,
as if the blond man had conjured it up, a cooling
wind came from the north. On its invisible streams
soared a huge hawk, as spectacular in wing span
and majesty as the new weapon they'd just wit-
nessed in action.

The smiles were plain to see now. One of the men,
unable to contain himself, strode over to the blond
man and wrapped him tightly inside an embarrassing
bear hug. The others soon gathered around the blond
man and congratulated him in less effusive ways.

The field where the demonstration took place was on
the eastern edge of the ranch where the blond man had
lived for the better part of the past year. After the guests
had seen what they came to see, the blond man led them
over to the stagecoach he'd rented for the day. Then all
of them climbed inside and went back to town, leaving
the blond man's assistants to wheel the weapon back in-

side the big, white barn that they'd fitted out as their laboratory.

Noah turned his pinto back toward the city, taking a narrow pass as a shortcut.

PART ONE

Chapter 1

In the worst of my drinking days, which was right after the war in which I'd been a Union spy and occasional assassin, I rarely looked forward to revisiting the saloon where I'd gotten drunk the previous night.

I was what people like to call a troublemaker. I argued, I belittled, I started fights for myself. I was even skillful enough in my red-eyed way to start fights for other people. Saloonkeepers were rarely happy to see me return. Many of them, in fact, told me I wasn't welcome and tossed my sorry ass out.

A four-day blackout got me off the bottle. I wish I could tell you that I had had a religious vision, or that I came to the philosophical conclusion that I was wasting my life, or that I realized how much more good, clean fun the sober life would be.

What it was, I'd never had a blackout that had stretched beyond thirty-six hours, and a four-day blank spot just plain scared the hell out of me. I woke up on a sunny Sunday morning in an alley in St. Louis, minus my Western boots, my Stetson, all my money, and all my identification. The last was the worst because, for an entire hour, I couldn't remember who I was.

I never did put those missing days together. When I remembered that my name was Noah Ford, that I was a field investigator for a branch of the United States Army, and that I was on assignment looking for two men who'd held up a train and unwittingly stolen some secret Army items, I wired Washington that I'd been kidnapped, tortured, and left to die. I therefore needed money immediately and new credentials to follow posthaste. I doubted they believed my story. They knew I was a drinker. But I captured 86 percent of the men they sent me after, so they decided to give me another chance.

The money came in seventy-two hours. The credentials took several days. I spent the time working for room and board at a convent. I painted the house the nuns lived in and then cleaned out an ancient barn that had bedeviled them since they'd moved in a year ago.

The first few days of sobriety were a lark. I kept thinking how easy this was going to be. I couldn't figure out why people complained about how hard it was to give up drinking. I didn't realize that I was having a sort of grace period. No anger, no fear, no irritation. Hard physical work that left me exhausted at the end of a ten-hour day, followed by good food, a bit of quiet reading in the attic of the convent, and then ten hours of sound sleep in a clean, sturdy bed.

But after my credentials came and I got back to my real work—which involved not only investigating, but lying, cheating, stealing, and even killing when necessary—then it wasn't so easy to walk past a saloon without feeling the shaky urge to take a drink, to hide inside the dark solace of drunkenness.

It was the sort of saloon where people who thought they ruled the world gathered to inflict their loud opinions on the expensive air.

You hear the same kind of loud alcoholic opinions shouted in deadfalls and cheap saloons, too, only not with quite the same air of certainty.

The name was the Founders Club and it was in the best section of town, far enough away from the raw wound of the small slum to make you forget slums altogether—which the members of the Founders Club had done a long time ago.

The blond man I'd seen demonstrate the machine gun earlier in the day sat with two of the men who'd seen the gun in action. I was inside the club because a retired colonel I'd known from the war had asked the club to serve me lunch here as a guest. They hadn't asked him any questions, which was fine, because he wasn't prepared to give them any answers.

The conversations I could overhear were about what you'd expect, most of the subjects gleaned from newspapers and magazines. New York City lighting every street with electricity. Canned fruits available coast to coast. Fifty thousand telephones in use across the country. The sort of things that interested businessmen. The only jabber that really caught my ear was about a gunfight in Tombstone, Arizona, at some corral. Who isn't interested in a gunfight story? A lot of them are bullshit, but if the teller of the tale

is good at his craft then the more bullshit the merrier,
I say.

I drank coffee until my small steak came. The
blond man didn't spot me until I'd been there fifteen
minutes. He did one of those double takes that stage
comedians like to do. From then on, whenever he
raised his gaze to look at me, he glared.

It took him an hour to get rid of the two men. At
the end there was a lot of handshaking and bicep-
patting and contrived smiling. They wanted what he
had, which was the weapon; he wanted what they
had, which was a great deal of money. It's interesting
to listen to all the praise on a man's lips turn to dis-
dain as soon as he's out of earshot of the man he's
been buttering up. We all do it but it ain't very pretty.

After they had disappeared into the cloakroom, he
came over and sat down. Neither of us spoke for a
while. He took a cigar from inside his suit coat,
snipped off the smoking end with a silver clipper, got
it lighted, and said, "Mother told me you were
dead."

"Well, you know good old Mom. Probably wish-
ful thinking on her part. She never did like me
much."

"Neither did Dad or our dear sister Claudene."

"How many husbands has our sister poisoned by
now?"

"You always were a cynical sonofabitch, Noah. I
suppose that's why you took up with the Yankees in
the war. They don't have any respect for tradition or
heritage and you don't, either. You had a good life on
the plantation and you turned your back on it."

"How many Yanks did you assassinate during the
war?"

"Near as I can figure, thirty."

"My last count was forty Rebs, including two colonels."

For the first time, he smiled. "We always were competitive."

"That's how they raised us, even though we didn't realize it until we were older. I don't miss them, David."

"Well, they don't miss you, either. In fact, nobody's permitted to utter your name in their presence."

The waiter came. My brother ordered whiskey. I ordered more coffee.

We gave the verbal jousting a rest. I silently noted his thinning blond hair, his dentures, his jowly but still handsome face. Just as he no doubt noted my crushed right ear, the twenty pounds I'd put on, and the occasional slight twitch of my gun hand, a memento of a day-long torturing by two female Reb spies who disabused me of the notion that females are necessarily more civilized than men.

He said, "I suppose I don't really hate you anymore."

"That's awfully white of you."

"You look sort of weary, actually. And I guess that makes me sad. I suppose you're still fighting the war."

"Half this country is still fighting the war. There're seditionist groups everywhere. The men you're dealing with—the arms dealers—at least two of them are seditionists. They figure if they blow up enough courthouses and trains that the South will rise again."

"Maybe it will."

"You know better than that."

He sighed. "Yes, I guess I do." He finished his drink. The familiar blue Ford eyes stared at me across the long melancholy years. We'd been loving brothers until the war had come along. Now we were nervous strangers. "You here to kill me, are you, Noah?"

"I'm here to get the gun back. You stole it from Mannering and then you killed Mannering. He invented it."

He shrugged. "One of my men killed him, actually. We took the gun from his laboratory. I was rifling his safe to get the papers for the designs. He got a gun somehow and tried to shoot me in the back. Got me high up in the left shoulder. I still don't have full use of my left arm. My man didn't have any choice. Killed him so he couldn't kill me. And, anyway, he'd only gotten the gun to a certain stage and didn't know how to go beyond it. I made the gun into a masterpiece."

"Humble as ever."

The waiter again. Another round.

"I don't have to kill you, David. Washington would be just as happy if I did—you've poached an awful lot of their experimental weapons the last few years—but I convinced them that Mannering's gun was more important than you."

"A true and loyal brother."

"Don't make me kill you, David."

The refreshments came. We sipped in silence for a time.

I said, "Why don't I get a buckboard and come back to your ranch house and pick up the gun?"

"Just like that, huh?"

"Just like that. Then you can do whatever the hell you want to do without any Federals on your back."

He took more of his drink. Set the glass down on the starched, virginal, white tablecloth. The whiskey looked rich auburn against the white. "I have kids and a wife to support."

"I know. Molly."

"A beautiful wife and an expensive wife. She's planning that we'll use the proceeds from the gun sale to spend a year in Europe. I haven't seen her in nearly a year. I want to bring her good news."

"I'm told you have a woman here."

A smile. "Gosh, imagine that."

The waiter. "Another, sir?" he said to David.

"Please."

"None for me," I said.

"Very good, sir."

When the waiter was gone, I said, "David, listen to me. Whatever else, we're brothers."

"Cain and Abel?"

"I wish I could find this as funny as you do."

"Then what? You take the gun and then arrest me for murder?"

"I'm going to give you a pass on the murder charge. A forty-eight-hour head start. And even after forty-eight hours, I don't plan to look for you very hard."

"I suppose I should say thank you, brother. But I'm not going to let you have the gun, Noah."

The waiter.

When we were alone again, I said, "Make this easy for me, David."

He didn't say anything.

Then, "It's my job, David."

"Ah, yes, your job. For President Grant. Good old Grant. I hear he drinks a touch. I hear he was quite courteous to General Lee when the South surrendered. That's the only time he treated us with any respect. Or don't you care how many of us died down there, Noah?"

I stood up. "I'll be there at sundown, David."

Chapter 2

Whenever I needed to pick up a couple freelance helpers, the first place I checked was the local stage line. They generally steered me to shotgun riders who worked part-time or had the day off. Given all the bank and stagecoach gangs working this part of Montana Territory, the shotgun men had to be good. And not be afraid of a little violence if necessary.

The Northeast Stage Line had a full house in back. Four coaches, everything from one of the new Concord models to an Abbott & Downing mudwagon to a pair of newly restored Deadwood stages that could carry eighteen passengers.

There had been some bad accidents with stagecoaches lately, the coach owners saying they were due to bad roads and acts of nature, the editorial writers saying they were due to drunk drivers and overworked horses. They were probably both right. Every coach in this lot had a small sign stuck on its doors: A RECORD OF SAFETY.

A man in a flat-crowned black hat, blue shirt, black trousers, and a small badge on the flap pocket of his shirt was talking to a youngster who was giving a muddy Concord a soapy wash with a bucket of water.

"Excuse me," I said.

The deputy took a photograph of me with his eyes and filed it away for future reference. That's a common trait in well-trained lawmen. He had a blandly handsome face and hard, dark eyes that made snap assessments of every human who walked or ran or crawled in front of their lenses. He didn't dislike me, his gaze revealed, but only because he didn't think I was worth bothering with.

"Morning," he said, "help you?"

"I'm actually looking for the boss."

He put forth a hand that was even harder than his eyes. "Frank Clarion. I'm a day deputy in town here."

"Nice to meet you, Clarion. Can you point me to the boss?"

"Right over there. And he's not only the boss, he's the owner."

"Tib Mason," the boy chimed in, wiping sweat from his face with the sleeve of his black-and-white-checkered shirt. "That's his name. He's my uncle. Same as the marshal's Mr. Clarion's uncle."

Now, I'm not one of those people who believe that it's necessarily a bad thing to hire your kin. I've known any number of father-son, uncle-nephew, cousin-cousin lawmen partnerships that work out just fine, even though most folks are automatically suspicious of them, suspecting nepotism and nothing more.

But Clarion's bland face tightened some when the kid mentioned that the marshal was Clarion's uncle.

He tried to make a joke of it. "Thanks for pointing that out, Merle."

Merle's bright-blue eyes dulled. He realized then that he'd said a bad thing, and that Clarion was going to kick his ass, verbally if not physically, as soon as he got a chance.

Having said the wrong thing many times in my own life, I tried to help the kid out a little. "I was a deputy once—and my uncle was the sheriff. Same setup as yours, Clarion. I imagine you get razzed about it sometimes as much as I did. But I did my best and got along just fine. And I'm sure that's how it works for you."

The dark gaze showed me a little more charity. Maybe I wasn't just another drifting saddlebum after all. Maybe I was a man of taste and discernment.

"Yeah," he said, and for an instant there he was almost likable, "they sure do like to kid you about working for your uncle."

Merle looked relieved. He went back to his washing with a smile on his freckled face.

"Nice to meet you," I said, and offered my hand to Clarion again.

Tib Mason turned out to be a short, beefy man in a tall, white Stetson, working a horse inside a rope corral. I walked over and watched him finish up with the animal. The paint wasn't much bigger than a colt. Mason kept everything gentle. He used his short whip only once, and then with obvious reluctance. When he saw me, he went up to the paint and stroked its neck several times, gentling it down. Then he walked over to me.

"If you're looking for Tib Mason," he said, "you found him."

"You're mighty nice to that paint."

"I like horses. We've got the best in the Territory on this line. And I personally tamed just about every one of them. And I didn't get mean with any of them." He took out his sack of Bull Durham, then his papers, and went to work. "So what can I do for you, mister?"

"Need to hire a couple of men."

"For what?"

I told him what I wanted him to know, which wasn't much. I also showed him my badge.

"They could get hurt."

"That's why I'm paying them so well."

"This Ford character out to that ranch. Nobody around here has much time for him. He made it plain that he didn't want anything to do with us. And we obliged him. We didn't want nothing to do with him, either." He got his cigarette lighted with a stick match and inhaled deeply. "He looks like he could be a tough sonofabitch."

"He is."

"You know him, do ya?"

"He's my brother."

He surprised me. He didn't look startled. He just grinned. "That'd probably make you just as strange as he is."

"It probably would."

Another drag. "How come you didn't go to the marshal and ask for some deputies?"

"Local law isn't always cooperative. We have to run the show and they resent that."

"You can't blame 'em for that, can you?"

"No, I can't blame them. But on the other hand, I need to do things the way the Army wants them done. I don't act on my own. I take orders."

He said, "How about me and a man named James Andrews? Full-blooded Cree. That kind of money, we'll do it. Just don't cheat him. He makes a bad enemy."

"Don't we all."

He shrugged. "I suspect you do. And I suspect your brother does. But that doesn't mean we're all like you, thank God."

"You'll go out to my brother's with me?"

"Sure. All those coaches you see over there—I owe the bank for every one of them. This should be some easy money for us."

I watched the paint before I spoke. He dug at the dirt with a long leg, as if he was going after buried treasure. He was young and strong. I almost hated to think of him spending his life on stage trails.

"Me and the Cree're good shots. And we're used to taking orders. The customers are our bosses. Same with folks we hire out to. You won't have any trouble with us. None at all."

"If he's Cree, why's his name James?"

"He shook his Stetson'd head. "Missionaries gave it to him. That's the name he prefers. I actually never heard him even say his Cree name."

"I'll need a buckboard."

"That won't be any trouble."

"And we'll meet here just about five? Buckboard and shotguns?"

"Fine by me, friend." He nodded to the paint inside the rope corral. "Better get back to work. He's getting restless."

I had supper just before four o'clock in a café that catered to townspeople of the merchant variety. You could deduce this from the headwear they wore, mostly homburgs. I was there for a steak and eggs. They were there for drinks.

I wasn't sure when or where he'd find me, but I knew he would. They come, of course, in different shapes, sizes, ages, dispositions. The canny ones choose a persona and pretty much stick to it. They can hide in the persona so that you can never guess their real thoughts or attitudes. Some strut like gunfighters; others kind of shuffle, trying to seem harmless; and some are crisp and curt, like bank managers who don't plan to give you a loan.

Then there is the grandfather school. When he came in the front door, several conversations paused, a couple of the waitresses froze in place momentarily, and the man you paid at the front counter put on a smile big enough to please a politician.

He wore no hat. Wouldn't want you to miss that head of long, pure white hair. Checkered shirt, somewhat wrinkled, the way a grandfather's would be. An inexpensive leather vest. Cheap gray trousers of the kind laborers wear. He had blue, blue eyes and a youthful grin, and the left hand he raised to wave with—there was a hint of the papal wave in it—was twisted just slightly with arthritis.

The badge he wore on the inexpensive vest was small. He wouldn't, being a granddad, want to give the impression of vanity or undue pride.

The corncob pipe was the nicest touch. No expensive briar for him. No, sir. Just a plain, ordinary, five-cent pipe, as befitted the good old trustworthy gramps that everybody knew and loved.

After he shook a few hands, the blue, blue eyes narrowed and lost a bit of their friendliness. He was hunting somebody. He was hunting me.

He fixed me with a gaze that would've made God tremble in his boots, and then he blessed the crowd with another sort of pope-like general wave (hell, he might have been absolving them of all their sins, the piss-elegant way he did it) and then he ambled over in my direction, pausing here and there for a few words with the men who worked hard at giving the impression that they were important, and probably were by town standards.

When he finally reached me, he said, "You mind if I sit down? I hate to bother you, but these old feet of mine are killin' me. And just about every table's filled up."

There were four empty tables in plain sight. But I knew he was going to sit down here anyway and so did he.

"Be happy for a little company," I said.

"Now that's mighty nice of you, friend."

A serving woman with a wide waist and a face full of freckles appeared with a schooner of beer, setting it down in front of the town marshal as if she'd been chosen to serve royalty. What was interesting and impressive about her behavior was that she seemed taken with the marshal out of respect, not because of fear. Which was the general reaction. That was to his credit.

When she left, he said, "Name's Wickham. Charley Wickham. I'm the town marshal."

We shook hands. "You seem to have a lot of friends."

"I'm not a bully and I generally don't hold

grudges. I give a lot of second chances, and if I get the opportunity to help a good man in bad trouble, I generally do it. I'm not a prude and I'm not a busybody. They've elected me to four two-year terms, and I expect they'll elect me a couple more times before I take my badge off this old vest of mine."

Now how the hell were you going to come back to that? There wasn't any brag in it, he was just stating what he saw were facts, and I had no doubt they were. If I lived here, I'd vote for him five or six times.

I hadn't told him my name. He said, "Now, Mr. Ford, you know and I know that I've checked you out and know that you're an investigator with the Army and that you've hired Tib Mason and James to go out to your brother's place at sundown. Now the thing is, I can keep right on going with this cornball bumpkin bullshit or I can cut right to it and ask you why the hell you didn't come to me before you looked up Tib. I could've gotten you a couple deputies and made it all legal."

"It is all legal, Marshal. I had a year of law school in Washington as part of my job. When Tib and James are with me, they're legal associates of mine. As long as what we do is legal, anyway."

"Tib tells me you were afraid I might not cooperate. Hell, Ford, I cooperate with every kind of investigator who comes through here, and that includes the Pinkertons, who can really get on a fella's nerves sometimes."

"Then I was wrong about you and I apologize."

He laughed. "I think we're quite a bit alike, Ford."

"Oh? How would that be?"

"You like to pretend to be all nice and reasonable and civil because you learned that that was the best way to hide what you're really after. Once a fella gets everybody all riled up, he's not gonna get his way except by force. And the only thing that force gets you eventually is dead. This town had four marshals in one year. You can find them up on the hill where the cemetery is. I had to apply three times for this job because they thought I was too quiet and gentle for it. I been marshal here for eight years now and in that time I've had to kill eighteen men, all of them white. But I didn't pick those fights, they did. I'm not especially good with a gun and I consider myself a serious coward. Every time I've been forced to shoot somebody, I spend a good hour puking my guts up afterward. I'm still scared of how close I came to dyin'. But what kept me alive is the one thing that none of those eighteen men had. And that was a calm temperament. Just like yours."

My food came and he said, "I'm going to let you eat in peace, Ford. But I just wanted to say that I'd appreciate you stopping by my office tonight and telling me how it went out at your brother's. I never have figured out what he's doing in that barn of his. He's got a Gatling gun that he fires a lot; his neighbors tell me that. But he's never given me or any of mine the time of day. Now all of a sudden here's this Army investigator who happens to be his brother going out there . . ."

He stood up. "You'd be curious, too."

"I sure would," I said, eager to start on my steak and eggs. "I'll stop at your place soon as I get back in town."

"I'd sure appreciate that." Then: "Tib and James." He made a sound not unlike a giggle. "Them boys is a pair of wild cards, let me tell you. Really wild cards."

Then he started working his way toward the front door, laughs and handshakes and back slaps for those he'd missed before.

Gramps.

Sure.

Chapter 3

Tib Mason sat in back with the shotguns. James rode on the seat with me. Autumn night came quickly. Frost gleamed on the prairie; shadows danced in the broken moonlight of the woods. An owl's cry followed us for some time.

There were flashes in the forest, mostly moonlight, but it was more fun to pretend the way the youngest soldiers used to, that the flashes were kin—grandfathers and dead brothers and maybe even sweethearts—risen fresh from the land beyond to soothe and comfort the scared and worn young troops who could no longer even remember what they were fighting for.

I hoped David had changed his mind. I suspected he didn't want a confrontation any more than I did. Which didn't mean, of course, that he wouldn't get involved in one if he had to. I had to convince him that he'd be free to walk away if he just gave me this gun. Neither of us would be foolish enough to think this would make him give up the kind of life he led.

Of course neither David nor others like him would

have been able to even learn about new weapons if the government wasn't so sloppy and corrupt.

The leak would have been in Washington. There was a good reason that President Lincoln had turned over all spy and espionage operations during the Civil War to the Pinkertons. It was because the Army could rarely keep secrets. Gun merchants, foreign and domestic, preyed on the Army people in the nation's capital. They used cash, sex, blackmail, whatever was required to pry secrets from the staffers back there. This didn't mean that they had any specific advance word of experimental weaponry, not usually. No, the cash, sex, and blackmail were used to trawl though the staffer's mind. He'd confide the number and nature of projects and they'd judge whether any of the projects sounded of interest to their sponsors. The men representing the gun manufacturers were mostly freelancers. If even one out of ten of the weapons proved desirable to their clients, a lot of money would be made.

The dusty road was pale gold. Road apples were heavy, thanks to stage traffic. Even with the railroad running full bore now, the stage in this part of the Territory was still used constantly. Every mile or so you'd see the lights of a tiny farmhouse. People had rushed here for gold. What didn't get talked about as much was all the people from back East who came here for several acres of land and a chance of communities better suited to their liking than the ones they'd happily left behind.

James said, "For my people, that is not a good sign."

I didn't have to ask what he was talking about. The icon of the ominous owl cut across a lot of racial and cultural lines. I'd spent three months in the Ozarks. The poor whites there had a whole legend of owls worked up. Some owls were good and some evil. I'd seen granny medicine reliant on scalding an owl to death in a huge, boiling kettle over a fire sprinkled with the bone dust of a raven. The scalded and seared juices of the owl were supposed to cure the cancer that had opened crater-like scabs on the neck of an old man.

"We'll be all right."

"Tib said there could be trouble. Trouble between brothers is not good."

"I'm hoping there isn't trouble, James."

Tonight he wore a dark headband to collect his long, gray-streaked hair. The buckskin shirt and trousers would keep him warm if there was a stand-off in the long, cold night.

From the bed of the buckboard, Tib said, "My old lady has a funny feeling about tonight. She didn't want me to come."

"If you'd feel better about it," I said, "you can drop off here. No questions asked, no hard feelings."

"You're an easy cuss."

"Not really. But if you're all spooked up, you're not going to do me much good. Same with James and the owl. If you're uneasy about this, James, I don't want you along, either."

Tib laughed. "Hell, sounds like you're tryin' to get rid of us. You ain't figured us out yet, Ford. We maybe don't look like it, but we're downright mercenary."

It usually works. Make fun of a man and his fears and he'll turn on you, tell you what a brave sumbitch he is and what a stupid sumbitch you are for doubt-ing his manliness.

"This is your call, Tib."

"You think we're pussies?" Tib said.

"I don't buy into owls and your old lady's spooked feelings, but I have to admit we don't know what we're riding into. Maybe my brother'll be reasonable and there won't be any trouble. Or maybe he's got a bunch of men there with carbines, just waiting to use them on us. There's always a chance we'll be outnumbered. That's something you have to take into account, I guess."

"I'm not a pussy." That white word in the mouth of a red man sounded kind of funny, like a little kid cussing. I smiled to myself.

"I sure don't think you are, James."

"Well, I sure ain't, either," Tib said.

"Never said you were, Tib."

Then Tib asked, "What exactly are we tryin' to get back from this brother of yours?"

"A gun."

"Must be some gun."

I didn't like or trust either of them. Couldn't explain it; just felt it. Maybe it was the way they were always glancing at each other. Their contempt for me was clear in the tone they took with me.

We reached the hill where I'd sat my horse earlier in the day. The night smelled of wood smoke and forest and snowy mountains. Fifty voices cried out their complaints, everything from baby birds to coyotes.

Now that it was dark, nothing was the same. A mountain wind had started ripping away the last of the remaining leaves. Shadows in crevices and gullies lent the landscape a mysterious, even treacherous, look. In daylight this area had been a sweet autumn land with apple trees and tilled acres and even a stream for fishing. But night wore a mask, and not a kind one. It could be hiding anything. I was an expert at night. I'd learned to use it pretty well back in the days of the war.

I grabbed my field glasses and stood up in the buckboard.

The house was dark. So was the barn. No sign of humans or horses. A couple of raccoons ate at spoiled apples in the backyard, their dark eyes gleaming whenever moonlight touched them.

James's breathing got heavier. The excitement of danger. Sometimes that made for the best kind of warrior; sometimes it made for the most reckless and foolish kind. I was beginning to get the sense that James belonged in the reckless category.

The three of us jumped down to the ground. Each of us toted a carbine, as well as a holster and sidearm.

"I can scout it for you," James said, confirming my sense that he was eager to get to the shooting, if there was to be any. And I guessed that if it didn't look like there would be any shooting, James would start some on his own.

"I appreciate that, James. But this is my fight. You're here for backup."

"That means what exactly?" Tib asked.

"Means I'm going down there and try to reason with him."

"Maybe they are gone," James said.

"Maybe. But I doubt it. He has men in this town who have money for him. He couldn't have made a deal that fast. We were supposed to meet and talk. That's what I hoped we'd do, anyway. Obviously, he had other ideas. We can't just pull our wagon up in the yard. We don't know what's waiting for us."

"He'd just shoot you down?" James said.

"I don't think so. But I can't be sure. We haven't spent a lot of time together since before the war. That's a long time ago. People change. That's the only thing you can count on."

Then: "You wait here," I said. "You've got my field glasses. You should have a pretty good sense of what's going on. I'll see you in a while."

I set off.

I swung west a quarter mile, into the loam-smelling woods, immediately entangled in under-brush as I sought some sort of trail. I found mud, feces, holes that tripped me, branches that lashed that broken face of mine, thorns that cut my hands, and at least half-a-dozen dead little critters that scav-engers of all kinds had had their way with.

I emerged at a fence line, barbed wire, and eased myself between two strands. There was no other way in. None, at least, any safer than this. I half-expected sniper fire to pick me off. Or at least try to scare me off, unless my brother had decided to make quick work of me. The only place to hide was the outhouse to the east. I kept listening for any human sound. There was always the possibility that Tib or James had inadvertently mentioned to somebody that we'd be coming to the ranch tonight. Or maybe not inad-vertently. It was pretty obvious that these two were the type who'd sell you to the highest bidder. Maybe they'd sold me out to David, and now David was waiting for me after setting the trap.

The ranch house had a shingle roof and adobe walls. Nothing moved in the dark windows; no smoke coiled from the tin chimney; no sound intruded on the silent yard. Sometimes you get a sense of places you're unfamiliar with. Some instinct allows you to take a reading. Danger or not danger. But I got no sense of the place. The house could be empty or there could be an army inside.

From here I couldn't see the front door, only the pine rear door. Ten feet away was the well. A small cross had been jammed into a tiny hill of dirt some time ago. A small animal of some kind. My brother and I had always been partial to animals. One of the quickest ways to be favored with a Ford punch in the face was to display any kind of cruelty to an animal.

I hefted my carbine. I told myself that I was estimating the amount of time it would take me to reach the back door from my present position. What I was doing was stalling, of course. I was thinking about what six or seven bullets tearing into me would feel like. I'd been wounded in the war. I didn't look forward to being wounded again. Even if I could trust David, I didn't know anything about the men with him. Maybe they'd shoot me and worry about David later.

But at this point, I wanted to get close enough to stand in front of him and make my case. It's a lot harder to shoot a man who's standing right in front of you. You have to take into account his humanity. Even the worst of us has a little bit of that left in us. I never assassinated anybody from close range. I couldn't afford to think of them as men with wives and children and lives. If I did, a lot of them would still be walking the earth. That was why I got sick of men on both sides bragging about the war. A lot of good men, wearing both colors, had died.

I crouched down and began a zigzag run toward the back door of the house. Even in the cool night, I was sweat-soaked by the time I ducked just below the doorknob. I was also out of breath, which was why for three or four full minutes, I just haunch-sat there, letting my body repair itself. I didn't need another reminder that I was no longer young. But there it was.

I reached up and put my hand on the doorknob. My fingers anticipated a mechanism that would not give. I was right. I spent five minutes on it.

I stood up, took several deep breaths. I was still sticky with sweat and my breathing was still somewhat ragged. I needed to piss, but now was not the time.

The door creaked and croaked as I opened it. I paused every time the door advanced an inch, expecting a blaze of gunfire. I planned to pitch myself to the ground left of the door at the first hint of trouble from inside.

But no such hint came.

The door was as noisy as one of those root cellar doors that remain closed for months at a time. Loud as coffin tops after a decade or two with the worms.

But no response from inside.

The interior was much larger than I'd assumed. Pale moonlight displayed good oriental rugs, solid furniture of mahogany and dark leather, even a few paintings more serious than big-eyed dogs and doe-eyed children covered the walls. The booze was of good quality; that would be David's doing, of course. Same with kitchen, both bedrooms and the workshop David had fashioned for himself on the large back porch—all neatly laid out and organized.

I went through drawers. I turned up nothing. The only things I found of note were photographs of David's children. There must have been twenty pictures. I'd had the sense that he'd left them behind mentally, as well as physically. But you don't keep this many pictures unless the kids are actively on your mind. Holding the photographs, seeing those sweet little earnest faces, I liked my brother much more than I had in years.

I heard something, or thought I did, and swung around, Colt ready.

The gray kitten with the tiny white paws looked at me and I looked at her. She mustn't have found me terribly interesting. She meowed once and then walked with a great deal of flounce and dignity out the back door I'd left open. She disappeared right through it.

I walked over to the window facing the yard. From there I had a good look at the rolling front doors of the barn. They were almost completely closed. There was maybe a foot between the two edges of them. Not so much as a glimmer of light from inside. The silence started to bother me again. It was unnatural. Maybe I'd guessed wrong. Maybe David had packed everything up and headed for the border. Now that he knew the Army was on to him, he might stay just across the Canadian border. He'd stayed there before. I needed to try the barn.

I took another walk-through of the house. It was one of those irrational acts you give into because you don't know what else to do for the moment. I'd searched it thoroughly. I wasn't going to turn up anything a second time through. And I didn't.

I went back to the window. I saw James and then Tib. They were making their way along the far side of the barn, keeping to the shadows of the chicken coop and a large shed. They were being careful, which told me that they probably hadn't tipped David off to me coming out here. If they were working with him they wouldn't have to worry about somebody spotting them and shooting.

They probably weren't all that brave. But they'd probably gotten bored sitting up on the hill waiting for something to happen. That's one thing you learn to fight against when you have to assassinate somebody. You have to wait them out till the moment's exactly right. A few minutes too early, a few minutes too late, can throw everything off. You might kill him all right, if you act too soon or too late, but you might blow your whole escape plan in the process.

The kitten had strolled out in front of the barn and now stood before the sliding doors, apparently watching James and Tib. I wanted to get those two the hell out of there. Any chance we had of sneaking in was likely gone now. Surely they'd been spotted by somebody inside the barn.

Maybe there was still time to wave them off. To proceed on the notion that they hadn't been seen. And then figure out a way to sneak into the barn myself. Maybe there was a haymow door in the back.

But for now I couldn't afford to clutter up my mind with thoughts. Now was time for simple action. To get them the hell out of there.

I got to the back door. Looked left, right, hefted

my carbine, proceeded along the back of the house as invisibly as I could. The moon didn't help. The roof didn't have but an inch or two of overhang. There were no deep shadows to hide in. The moon was like a huge cosmic lantern. If a shooter had a bead on me, the moonlight made me easy pickings.

There was a stubby oak tree to the east of the barn. I crouched behind it and picked up a few small pebbles. I'd never been much of a pitcher in baseball. But I could throw well enough to get their attention. I launched the first, then the second, of the pebbles.

I got Tib on the arm. The way he spun around, the way his face went startled and ugly, the way his gun sought out somebody to unload on—all these responses in just a second or two. I stuck my face out for him to see. You could almost feel his rage and curiosity drain away. He waved. I waved back.

James saw what he was doing. His eyes narrowed and looked for me in the gloom around the trees. He saw me. Scowled. He was ready for action and I was stopping him. If he didn't get action soon, maybe he'd turn on me.

I waved them off again. They nodded, understanding quickly what I wanted them to do. To fade into the trees behind them. Tib went quickly. James lingered in the moonlight. He wore a big frown. By not moving, by glaring at me, he was challenging my authority. He would be thinking that I was some Federale from the East and what the hell did I know about how things were done out here in the West and I wasn't paying him all that much money, anyway, and just why the hell was he taking orders from me, anyway? Plus, at some point or another he'd also be thinking about the gun itself. David's gun. The entire focus of my trip and the four arms merchants who wanted it. James had to be at least daydreaming how much money could be his if he could somehow steal the gun for himself.

But he relented. Shook his head in disgust and then turned toward Tib and started walking.

From the chicken coop came a sudden cacophony of excited hens. Maybe a dustup of some kind. Chickens certainly had a sullen temperament. The noise was raw on the silence. Usually chickens sounded sort of comic. But tonight there was something threatening in their anger. They battled there for what seemed a long, long time. But I used the distraction. If David was in the barn, the fighting in the chicken coop would distract him just as much as it distracted me.

It took me ten minutes to get behind the barn. I was sweaty again, shaky. I also had the feeling once more that at least one pair of eyes was watching me. Amused, maybe, but with that power hidden observers always have—the ability to surprise you. The ability to do just about any damned thing they want if they're clever or nasty enough.

There was no haymow door in the back of the barn. There was a single, small door but it didn't offer much hope to an intruder. The barn was big, but not big enough to allow anybody to open a door without being heard. I hunched down and walked around to the side of the barn. A small hatch sat very near the eave of the roof. With a good rope I could probably climb up the side of the barn and climb in through that hatch. But I didn't have a good rope, now, did I? Not even a bad rope, for that matter. And there was the noise problem again. Even if I reached the hatch, they'd probably hear me when I opened it.

I did the only thing I could. I crouched behind a hay wagon, watching the back of the barn as if it had some secret to reveal to me. But tonight it was keeping its secrets to itself.

I decided to find Tib and James and see if between the three of us we could figure out some way to get me into the barn. It was funny, hunched down this way, the barn so near and familiar. A barn was a barn. But not this one. For all its familiarity—I saw barns just like it every day—there was still that unknown quality about it. That menacing quality. Maybe it was knowing the gun was inside.

I worked my way around the far side of the grassy land to the tree line and then stayed to the shadows, trying to find Tib and James who were, presumably, anyway, hiding somewhere in the near oaks and hardwoods. The silence was on the land again. For thirty seconds there not even one of the night birds sang or cried. The barn loomed more ominous than ever, a kind of forbidden quality to what was nothing more than a stack of two-by-fours, nails, and white paint.

A familiar feeling from my war days came back. Isolation. Three of us had been trying to sneak into the house of a Confederate general whose grown daughter was working as a spy for her father. She was known to be home for a few weeks. She was also known to have seduced a Union Army captain out of some important battle plans. We wanted to know who she'd shared those plans with. The back of the mansion sat along the edge of a river. We reached it by raft. Now we were coming up on the mansion itself. I was, anyway. When I glanced over my shoulder, I realized something was wrong. The two men working with me had stayed below on the raft. I hurried back to the small cliff above the river. When they saw me, they started laughing and pointing to something behind me. I felt isolated in a way I never had before. The world had completely turned around on me. The two men working with me were double agents. And I guessed correctly that behind me now I'd find one or two soldiers with rifles pointed at my back.

I had that sense again. Isolation. Was I the only person in the entire world?

"Hey! Here!" Tib stage whispered.

And damn I was glad to hear another voice.

The woods did a damned good job of hiding them. Not even the moonlight exposed them. They couldn't have been much more than a few feet inside the shifting shadows of the woods, but I hadn't seen them until Tib spoke up. I eased my way between two hardwoods and some oaks.

James told me that he'd climbed up in a tree for a better look at the barn. He hadn't seen or heard anything. He said he still didn't think the barn was empty but Tib just shook his head and said it was, the Indian was crazy.

Everything we said was in whispers, three men huddled together on a sandy little trail.

"Nothing in the house?" Tib asked.

"Nothing."

"Then they're in the barn," James said.

"If they're here."

"You thinkin' they're gone, Noah?"

"Considering it. I didn't think so at first. But it's

awful damned quiet. You said you didn't hear anything. I didn't, either."

Tib said, "Even if they're gone, we still get paid, right?"

"Hell, yes," I said.

"Just checkin'." I must've sounded harsh to Tib.

"I want you two to find an angle on the front door. Then open fire. That'll give me cover to get into the barn the back way."

"Why not just sneak in the back door without no gunfire?" Tib said.

"Good chance they'd hear me. I need to surprise them."

"If anybody's in there," James said, "I guess we'll know pretty fast."

"We should get closer than these woods, if we're going to do any good," Tib said. "Then we'll just make a run at the front doors. Soon as you hear us shootin', that's when you head for the back door. Is that right?"

"Right," I said.

I was getting suspicious again. They didn't seem bothered by charging the front door of a barn that could very well be hiding a powerful new kind of weapon and maybe three or four men besides. Maybe they were just eager for action, or maybe the people inside the barn—if there were any—were in on the whole ruse.

James said, "We can sneak up on the barn from an angle, pepper the front doors, but be in a place where they can't get us with their guns. There ain't no windows on this side of the barn. They want to hit us, they'll have to come out of the barn to do it, and I doubt they'll do that."

"All right," I said. "Give me a few minutes to get to the back of the barn. Then you open fire. You ready?"

Tib said, "I'll count to a hundred and then we'll start shootin'."

I backtracked pretty much the same way I'd come. I tried to keep any noise down, not only so they wouldn't hear me, but so I could hear them if they made any sound. If they were in there, they sure knew how to wait somebody out. Not a sound. And by this time, the chickens and the roosters had long been quiet, too. We were back to the wind crying in the spare autumn trees.

I found the hayrack and crouched behind it. Soon as the gunfire started I'd sprint over to the door.

I started to wonder if something had gone wrong. Tib had had plenty of time to count to a hundred, but still there was no gunfire. A coyote, loud and lonely; night birds crying, entangled in the maze of the woods. But no gunfire.

Finally, it came. Harsh and harrowing on the air. Tib firing his six-gun, James firing his carbine.

I used the noise and the time to race to the back door of the barn. Weather had warped the wood so that the door had swollen tight against the frame. I reached behind my back for my knife. I'd have to slit the swell open sufficiently to pull the door wide enough to slip through.

I didn't notice it at first, the fact that there'd been no response whatsoever. I was too busy with my knife.

But Tib brought my attention to it by yelling loud and clear: "Yipee! C'mon around and walk in the front door like a white man, Noah! Nobody's home!"

I wasn't sure how I felt about that. Nobody's home

meant that I wouldn't have to confront my brother. But nobody's home meant that the experimental gun—the only one like it—was on the open market; David was gone. Once again the gun was open to bids from foreign governments that meant us harm. (The State Department had heard whispers that Germany had had "informal" talks with Mexico about someday invading America with German help, giving the Germans a sure foothold on this continent.)

"Be there in a minute!" I shouted.

I slid my knife back into its scabbard, grabbed my carbine. I heard James laugh about something and then Tib laugh, too.

I'd taken maybe three or four steps, still pretty far away from the rear corner of the barn, when the world came to an end.

That was what it sounded like, anyway. All the rage and commotion I'd heard when David had demonstrated his gun in a few short bursts for his visitors was quadrupled in the fury that ripped the night now. This was David's gun put to full power. Somewhere in the tumult of the bullets tearing from his experimental weapon I heard the screams of James and Tib.

My mind formed an instant picture of them. Their faces stricken with the knowledge that death had set upon them, their arms and legs flying in contrary directions, their screams so startled that they weren't even real screams—just choked, gasping sounds exploding from their throats.

That was my last thought: James and Tib are dead. The machine gun turrets were relentless. And now they were turned on me, the bullets ripping through the weathered wood of the barn.

And then I had no other thought at all because I felt several bullets tearing into me. I had just time enough to make my own screams; just enough time to feel my own arms and legs fly in contrary directions; just enough time to feel my own death set upon me.

Chapter 4

The mayor of a prosperous Colorado town once told me that the mark of a town that was going somewhere was twofold. First, it got itself an important railroad connection, and then it got itself a hospital with at least two doctors who'd graduated from an accredited medical school.

I woke up in a white room made even whiter by the late morning autumn sunlight. A squirrel sat on the ledge of my window, as curious about me as I was about it. The pain in my upper back made even the slightest movement difficult, but somehow I was able to fasten my full attention on the nervous squirrel. I like to think that we exchanged smiles of a sort but that, I realize, was probably drugged-up nonsense.

I lay there listening to the hospital sounds. After the war I'd visited a number of friends in the big vets' hospital in Washington, D.C., the one where they dealt with the amputees. The same faces told conflicting stories—happy to be alive, resentful that they'd never be whole again. Some of them adjusted pretty damned well, considering—probably a lot better than I would have—but some of them were headed to angry, bitter lives with the whiskey bottle their only consolation. I didn't have any bitterness or conflict of feelings. Wherever I was exactly, I was happy to be alive.

She came through the door in a uniform as crisp and white as her personality. A slender blonde wearing a shy smile on her pretty, melancholy face. She carried a tray with three small bottles of medication on it. She brought it to the table next to my bed and said, "I understand that you've already talked to the doctor."

"He didn't tell me much."

"Well, there isn't that much to say, really."

"A bullet in my right shoulder."

"That's right. And you picked up a very high fever from the infection."

She was a pillow-fluffing, bedclothes-straightening, fresh flower-arranging whiz. Most impressively, she could talk even while doing all this. I suppose I was more impressed with her skills than I should have been, but then I was only half alive and she was awfully damned pretty. I'd also noticed that she wasn't wearing a wedding ring. I fixed her at midtwenties.

"I'd really like to change your sheets. You sweated through them."

"Fine with me."

"I'll have to have you sit in a chair. It'll hurt."

"I'll give it a try."

I tried being stoic about it all, the way men are supposed to be. Even though I nearly blacked out twice, I held my response to the pain of sitting up to a few choked-off grunts and groans.

"You're a strong man, Mr. Ford."

"I was hoping you'd say that."

She blessed me with a smile. As she stripped the bed and wiped down the rubber sheet beneath with disinfectant, she said, "Women like to hear they're pretty and men like to hear they're tough."

"You must hear 'pretty' a hundred times a day."

"A hundred would be a slight exaggeration." She wasn't facing me, but I could feel her smile. "But you're running a fever so I'll let it go this time."

In a few minutes, I had a fresh new bed. I was holding as tough as I could but I was getting groggy. The fever was making me fade in and out of awareness. She got me back into bed and said, "You need to sleep."

"Yeah. I think you're right." Then: "Tell me something."

"What?"

"You said that doc who came in this morning—if he told me how I got here, I don't remember."

"I'm told you were brought here by the marshal and two of his deputies."

"All I can remember was hearing Tib and James start screaming. You know who they are?"

"I'm sorry, they're both dead."

"You know anything more than that?"

She laid a cool, work-roughened palm on my forehead. "You're burning up. Let me give you something for that and then you get some sleep. The marshal said he'll be here late morning."

"So you know what happened last night?"

"A little bit about it. Not much. The marshal said not to talk to you about anything."

"You afraid of him?"

The smile. She had the kind of slightly crooked teeth that are attractive. "Not afraid of him. But I like him and so I'll do what he asks."

The pain was starting to black me out every couple moments.

And then I realized how bad off I was. I'd been awake here for maybe ten minutes and I remembered that Tib and James were dead, but I'd forgotten all about the person who mattered most.

"My brother David . . ." I started to say.

This time her smile was completely mechanical. She pulled my covers up to my chest and said, "The marshal will tell you everything when he gets here."

"He's dead, isn't he?"

"Please don't put me in the middle of this, Mr. Ford."

"Just tell me the truth. Then I won't ask you any more questions. My brother—he's dead, isn't he?"

She sighed. "Yes, Mr. Ford. I'm afraid he is."

She turned and walked out of the room.

I lay awake for what seemed a long time. I was so exhausted from the wound that I didn't feel the news as sharply as I might have otherwise. It was a fact more than a feeling. My brother David was dead. So many memories, good and bad, and yet these, too, were pictures that didn't bring with them any particular emotion. Maybe I was willing myself not to feel anything. Maybe my body knew, even if my mind didn't, that to deal with David's death directly would weaken me even further. I thought of my parents, too, and how each of them would handle the news. Once they learned that I was involved, they'd wonder if I had a hand in his death. They would try not to think the worst of me because that suspicion, along with the reality of his death, would simply be too much for them to reckon with. But they would say—or at least think—that now both their sons were dead. And even though that wasn't literally true, it was spiritually true to them. I'd perished a long time ago.

"I wish you'd have let me go along with you. Or asked me to let Frank here join in."

Marshal Wickham opened with these words. They were about what I'd expected. It's hard for most of us not to say I told you so.

But in this case I had to disagree. "My brother's dead. The whole point of it was keeping him alive. I guess he didn't care about living as much as I thought he did. Tib or James must've gotten lucky and shot him before they died."

Deputy Frank Clarion stood next to his uncle and said, "I'm not a great shot, but I could've helped." The dark eyes hinted at a friendliness I hadn't seen the other day at Tib Mason's stage line. "We like folks to enjoy themselves when they come here. Even Federal agents. Hell of a way to spend your time here." Then, as if realizing that this wasn't the time for humor, he said, "I'm sorry about your brother."

"Thanks. I appreciate that."

He nodded to the marshal and said, "Well, I better go check the mail and see if there's anything I need to take care of."

When he'd gone, Wickham said, "A lot of people think I hired him because he's my kin. My sister's a widow and she had to raise him alone and he got into his share of trouble. But I'll tell you, he's turned out to be a damned good deputy, no matter what people might say."

"He sure seems like it."

He pulled a chair up to my bedside. He'd walked into the sunny room bearing a cup of coffee in one hand and his corncob pipe in the other. Once he was seated, he fired up the pipe, took a sip of his coffee and said, "How you feeling?"

"Fine and dandy."

"How was it that damned gun didn't cut you down, too?"

"I was trying to sneak in the back way. David opened up through the front of the barn." I'd had some food, some coffee, and most importantly, some sleep. Last night was reshaping itself in my mind. I kept wondering how Tib or James had managed to kill David. Unless they'd hit him when they'd fired into the barn when they were hoping to spook up some kind of response.

"That the big mystery your brother was working on? The gun?"

"Yep."

"There're four men over to the hotel who won't talk to me. You have any idea who they are?"

I made the mistake of trying to shrug. Pain stopped the gesture instantly. "Not by name."

He studied me. "Not by name—then by what?"

"I'm not sure I want to bring you in on this. I was thinking of wiring St. Louis. Bring a couple of the brass up here to help me work on this."

He leaned back in his chair. Gramps. His white hair was almost ghostly in the sunlight. "Way ahead of you on that one. I wired the territorial governor and explained that you were wounded and that I needed to get involved in this right away so no time would be wasted. He's wiring the Department of the Army right now. I expect they'll tell him that I can proceed." A tug on his pipe. "So you might as well tell me what the hell's going on here. First of all, what was your brother doing on that ranch for nearly a year?"

Flashes of memory. David and I playing cowboys and Indians. David taking his stupid horn lessons and me making fun of him. Me jumping him from this hiding place I had in the tree near the line of forest on our plantation. David and I with our father on the steamboat trips he used to treat us to.

Wickham watched me. He obviously sensed what I was feeling. "I lost my brother when he was ten. He'd strayed off the farm. Tornado came and a tree crushed him. I still can cry about it. Sometimes I won't even be aware I'm thinkin' of him. I just start cryin'. It's a terrible thing to say, but I don't even do that for my poor wife, God rest her soul. Cry like that, I mean."

If he was using a dead little brother—if he even had a dead little brother—to convince me that we shared the same kind of loss and therefore that made us kin of a kind—well, it worked.

"You can trust me, Ford."

"I guess I'll have to."

This time he took coffee instead of the pipe. "I'd appreciate it if you'd tell me as much as you're up to. The doc only give me fifteen minutes with you. Those four men I mentioned. They were here several months ago. I pretty much figured out they were some kind of contraband agents."

So I told him. As a story, it was a simple one. Six,

seven sentences and you pretty much had it. Brother David lost his plantation and everything else in the war. Became a thief who usually dealt with arms that could be sold for big money to arms merchants, domestic and foreign.

"That a big business?" This was the only time he interrupted me.

"Between foreign powers that want to be more powerful and seditionist groups that still believe the war is going on and average, everyday thugs who want to move up in the world—it's a huge business."

"Dangerous, too."

"Well, he got killed, didn't he?"

His expression changed. "There's something you need to know, Ford. And that's why I told those four men that they can't leave town until I give them permission. I told the fellas down to the train depot and the fellas over to the stage line and the fellas over to the livery that if any of them try to go anywhere, they're to run to my office and let us know immediately."

"Kind of people they are, I'm surprised they were so cooperative."

"Either that or I told them they'd spend their time in jail. These're city slickers we're dealing with." He smiled. "Idea of them spending three, four nights in a hick-town jail tickles the hell out of me—but it sure don't do much for them. So they cooperated."

"Do any of them have the gun or know what happened to it?"

"I'll get to that in a minute. When I leave here I'm gonna give you all the things I got from talkin' to them. Spent about an hour each with 'em. Wrote it down in pencil and had my office lady print it up on that noisy damned machine we got in the front office. You're gonna need another rest here pretty soon. But when you wake up, I'd like you to look these things over. Maybe it'll help us figurin' out who killed him. I'm pretty sure one—or a couple of them together— were the ones who killed him."

"But I told you—Tib and James fired a lot of shots into the barn."

"Wasn't bullets that killed him."

"What the hell do you mean?"

He sucked on his pipe, but it had gone out. "Somebody cut your brother's throat, Ford, and did a hell of a bloody job doing it."

I slept the rest of the day. It was an automatic response, I suppose, to David being dead. We mourn those we love; that's sad enough. But to mourn somebody you loved, yet at times hated—that's even sadder, because one feeling corrupts the other. But there wasn't a whole hell of a lot I could do about it. I was pretty sure he'd felt the same about me.

I was awakened by the day's-end rush. Staff people saying goodbye to each other; trays of food being delivered to the sixteen patients in the place; early visitors to see family members. You could smell dinner coming. Weak as I was in some respects, I sure had a good appetite. I sipped some water and then made my first struggling attempt to roll and light a cigarette one-handed. By the time I had a lumpy white cylinder rolled, I had spilled a third of the Bull Durham pouch on the nightstand and torn four cigarette papers. A wizard I wasn't. I didn't fare much better with the matches. I burned the hell out of my thumb. The flesh around it was now brittle and brown, and the nail itself gray from the match heads.

The smoke tasted good. I took it down deep and true, and when I expelled it, it looked gas-jet blue in the sunlight. A nurse peeked in to say see you tomorrow, Mr. Ford, and the woman who'd cleaned the room asked if I was done with the magazines I'd told her she could have. I told her sure. She said her daughter would be very excited.

I had succumbed to the pace of the hospital. You can fight it, but why bother? Either your wound or illness or the sheer monotony of the place will get you eventually, anyway.

I concentrated on the method of David's death rather than his death itself. I'd be working through my regrets about his passing the rest of my life.

For now, I wanted to know who had cut his throat and why. The automatic assumption was that one of the men he had working with him had killed him to take the gun and sell it. Maybe two or three of them together had done it.

The next assumption was that one of the four men who'd come to buy the gun had done it, one of the men the marshal had told to stay in town.

The smell of hot food was welcome, even if it turned out to be only the usual broth and bland slice of white bread, served with a small cup of vegetable soup. What I'd been picturing was something more along the lines of a slab of beef and boiled potatoes and some kind of vegetable with a slice of cherry pie and hot black coffee, chicory flavor, if you have it, ma'am, for dessert.

The hefty night nurse must have caught my expression. "You'll be eating regular tomorrow. The doctor told me to tell you that. Man like you wants food. Now you lay back there."

She fed me. I dribbled a lot. I supposed it was undignified, but I didn't give a damn. I'd seen too much in the war to care about dignity. I'd seen men— mostly young men who could have been my sons or nephews—puking, shitting, sobbing, begging, screaming when they died to believe anymore in dignity. Dignity wouldn't have helped those kids, anyway, and I mean both sides. I'm not one of those braying winners. Both sides suffered far too much to brag about anything.

When I'd sufficiently fouled my chin and the bib the nurse had wisely slung around my neck, I said, "There was a nurse this afternoon . . ."

And that was as far as I got.

"Jane Churchill."

"How'd you know the one I meant?"

"All the men ask about her."

"Ah."

"She's a pretty one, isn't she?"

"Very."

The woman laughed. She had a round, wise, pleasant face. "They're always sending her birthday cards and things like that. Christmas cards, too." She took my bib away and then started wiping my face with a damp, soapy cloth. "But I'm surprised she didn't tell you."

"Tell me what?"

"Who she is. She used to spend time with your brother. He was quite the dancer, you know."

"David?"

"Um-hm. You'd see them together out to the barn

dances. People loved to watch them dance. And they figured that they were right for each other—she keeps to herself just the way that brother of yours kept to himself."

Back when we were kids, David would never dance at any of the local festivities. He always said that dancing was for girls. I smiled at the picture of him leading a pretty girl around on the floor. And in the case of Nurse Jane . . . she was quite the pretty girl.

"You didn't know that, huh?"

She was getting everything ready for tonight. Plumping pillows, straightening sheets, setting a fresh pitcher of water on my nightstand.

"They went out and everything?" I said. Had she known he had a wife?

"If you mean courted, I guess you'd call it that. She visited him a lot at the ranch he rented, anyway. People talked, both of them being unmarried and everything. But then you know how people do. They make something dirty out of everything, just so they'll have something to talk about. Live and let live, I say."

"Well, I'm with you," I said in a stout, half-kidding voice. "If people want to defile each other in the middle of the road, I say, durn well let 'em."

She poured me a glass of water.

"Now you're making fun of me."

"No, I'm not. Just fooling around a little."

"I don't mind admitting that I wish men treated me the way they treat her."

"You mean Jane?"

She nodded. "Just to go through life one day the

way she does. Having all these men treat her so special and everything."

Her voice was genuinely wistful. A middle-aged woman and a fond daydream. I liked her and felt sorry for her. Life is an awfully random process when you come right down to it, and the nice people don't always get the reward they deserve. A lot of ugly folks are awfully nice, and a lot of beautiful ones aren't. Then again, some ugly ones are pretty vile and some beautiful ones are gentle and kind and good. Figuring out life tends to give me a headache sometimes.

"But I'm just jealous."

"Nothing wrong with that. You're just human, is all."

"I suppose. But I always feel that I should grow up someday and not let things like that bother me."

I took her wrist, gently. "An old priest in the war told me something. He said that after hearing a couple thousand confessions, he'd figured out that nobody ever really grows up."

Her whoop of a laugh was almost like the note of a song perfectly sung. "Now, that one I'll have to remember."

"Don't you think it's true when you think of it? You look at people from the outside and they can look really old, but you listen to them and they're basically the same as they were when they were younger—the same anger and pleasure and fear. We're all kids hiding out in these adult bodies."

"I'm going to quote you on that."

"That's what the old priest said. Not me. I'm not smart enough to say things like that."

"I'll just bet you're not," she said.

Then she was gone and then it was night. She came in later and asked me if she should turn up my lantern. I said no. I wanted the darkness. David, dancing. David and the nurse named Jane. I found myself resenting him again. And without quite knowing why.

Chapter 5

DENNIS WAYLAND—ASSOCIATED WITH GERMAN EMBASSY IN NEW YORK

THOMAS BRINKLEY—REPRESENTATIVE OF THE KRUGER ARMS COMPANY, BELEURS, KENTUCKY, PROMINENT COPPERHEAD

LEE SPENSER—FREELANCE ARMS DEALER

GILES FAIRBAIN—STAFF MEMBER, SENATOR LAWTON CAINE

I woke up much earlier than I wanted to. From the gray sky, I guessed it was an hour or so before dawn. There wasn't much to do except turn up the lantern and go over the files Marshal Wickham had left me.

I was glad he'd had them typed up. Wickham had scribbled a note to me on the corner of a page and it took me five minutes to decipher his handwriting. What it said was, "Be interesting to see your reaction to these fellas."

I spent nearly two hours with the eight typed

pages. There was nothing remarkable about any of them as far as occupations went. The international arms cartel is made up of freelancers working for countries they won't name, men who work for a handful of foreign embassies in New York and Washington, and even for senators who are secretly working for one branch of service or the other. The competition between the Army and the Marines, for example, is almost equal to that between fighting countries. Senator Caine was a West Point graduate; there was no doubt about his sympathies. The rest of the information Wickham had given me was just as interesting and just as useless. At least on the surface.

You have to wonder about people who deal in arms, wonder if they've ever been in a war, ever seen what guns do to people. Big guns, small guns, it doesn't matter. There were battles on both sides where the dead had been piled up like cordwood. You never smelled anything like it before. Or saw anything like it, either, after the crows had bloodied their beaks with the eyes of the dead men.

Countries always claimed to detest war. If one somehow got started, they claimed it wasn't them who started it, it was that other country. And if they took the blame for starting it, why, they only did so because, they claimed, the other country would have invaded them anyhow at some point in the future.

Even the countries that claimed neutrality were rarely neutral. They made dirty secret money on wars, either banking millions for tyrants who planned to flee if the war went badly, or being middlemen for the arms merchants.

Jane came in just before six o'clock.

She'd been laying out pills on my nightstand. She

didn't look up. In the lamplight her features were soft and sentimental, like one of those idealized sweet women on magazine covers.

"I should've said something. About David and me."

"Yeah. I guess you should've."

"I just didn't know how to bring it up. Given— your relationship with him."

When our glances met, she said, "Marshal Wickham told me that they went through his things and found that he was married."

So she hadn't known.

"I don't like to think of myself that way." Then: "As an adulteress."

The word sounded pretty severe on her tongue.

"You weren't an adulteress. You didn't know he was married."

She was near enough to touch my good shoulder. "I appreciate you saying that. But it still makes me feel dirty. He had a wife waiting for him."

"Not much of a wife, from what he said."

We went through the process of her changing my sheets again. "Your temperature's back to where it should be. The pills took care of the infection."

"I feel better. Not great. But better."

"We're going to try you in a wheelchair. This company wants to sell us two of them so they gave us one to try out."

When we finished with the sheets, I lay back. She stood next to my bed and washed my face and hands with a damp cloth.

"He talked about you sometimes."

My laugh was as harsh as my words had been. "I can imagine."

"He cared about you, actually."

For the first time—probably because I was getting stronger and more aware of things—I detected a faint British accent in her voice.

"How long have you been in the States?"

She smiled. "The accent? I came here when I was seven. I've still got traces of it. Now let's deal with the pills. You've got eight of them this morning."

We didn't talk while she set one pill after another on my tongue. One of them gagged me and I had to sit up abruptly. All the pain came back. So did an instant headache.

I lay back. She put a cool, damp cloth on my head. "I imagine that hurt."

I closed my eyes, rested a moment. "You know who killed him?"

"No. I'm afraid not. Marshal Wickham asked me the same thing."

She looked sad and old in that moment. Even frail. "Now that I know that he was married—that he lied to me all this time—I don't know what to think. About him or myself."

I reached out and took her hand. "You're being too rough on yourself. Like I said, you didn't know." Then she did something that probably surprised both of us. She leaned down and kissed my forehead. It wasn't a romantic kiss. It was a fond kiss. But it made me feel idiotically happy. She was such a clean, fine woman; the kind of woman who'd never paid any attention to me at all; the kind of woman my brother had gone through with ease.

"Maybe I should've been curious. Should've asked." Then: "I need to get to work. The chamber pot for one thing."

"You get all the good jobs."

"I don't mind. I like helping people."

But she lingered there. Thankfully. "It makes me feel as if I'm doing something with my life. Helping people. David used to laugh when I said that. And I suppose it does sound a bit too noble. But it has to do with my background, I suppose."

"In England?"

She nodded. "I spent my girlhood with servants. Then my father lost his money in some African diamond ruse and we were out on the street. My father had alienated everybody in his family while he was rich. He was a very arrogant man. I loved him without liking him, if you know what I mean by that. My sister, who got the looks, married a lord, and made the transition with no difficulty at all." She laughed. "As near as I can figure it, Nanette was poor for about three hours. Father and I moved to London. He'd trained as a barrister but had never practiced in any serious way. My mother had died a few years before that. She was a very dear woman. I'm glad she didn't live to see us lose our money. I went to nursing school and studied hard so I could graduate early. Father ended up working in a men's clothing store in Carnaby Street. He had to wait on men he'd once been socially superior to. It wasn't easy for him. We had a gas stove in our little flat. He used it to kill himself one winter's night. I never even cried about it. I believe in an afterlife, so I believe he's in a better place now." That melancholy half-smile again. "If there was one man who was not cut out to be poor, it was Father. Believe me. I lost myself in my nursing. When you help other people you tend to forget about your own problems. So I suppose David was right. It's not noble at all. It's selfish. You help others so you can forget about yourself."

"I guess that's true. But the point is, you help other people. It doesn't matter why you do it." I reached up and touched her slender forearm. "There's one point in your story I had a little trouble with."

"Oh? Which point was that?"

"That your sister got the looks."

She laughed, sounding genuinely surprised. "That's very flattering. But believe me, if I was standing next to Nanette right now, you wouldn't even notice me. I'm attractive in my way, but she's beautiful. I was only half-joking when I said she was poor for only about three hours. Rich men were throwing themselves at her."

Then she was straightening my sheet, tucking me in. "Take yourself a little nap, then we'll let you terrorize the hospital in that wheelchair."

My people have always been crazed for contraptions. My father always had to be the first one to own just about any given contraption he heard about. We had the first player piano, the first typewriting machine, the first machine-made watch, the first safety lift, and the first internal combustion engine.

What Jane wheeled into my room was the first true wheelchair I'd ever seen. The last time I'd visited the vets' hospital in D.C., a couple of the docs were talking about a company that was experimenting with building a wicker chair and putting bicycle tires on the sides of it so that the chairbound person could wheel himself around. Previous chairs had been just that—chairs with caster wheels on the bottom that could be pushed from behind by a nurse or friend.

What I was looking at gave the chair-sitter a whole lot of mobility. On a flat surface he could go where he wanted without any assistance.

"You should see yourself," Jane said. "You look as excited as a little kid."

"The family curse. Contraptions."

"That's how David was about guns." When she mentioned his name, her eyes got sad for a moment. She probably hadn't figured out which hurt more—his death or his deceit.

"You could have races in these things."

It was good to see her smile. "I'm not sure that's what they have in mind for these. But yes, little boy, I'm sure you could race in these if you really wanted to. Why don't I help you out of bed so you can try it out?"

I surprised myself when I stood up. Not dizzy. Not weak. The shoulder hurt all the way down into my elbow. But it was pain at a tolerable level, not pain that distracted you or made you want to crawl back in bed.

"I think I'm on the mend."

"Well, then, maybe you won't want to try this," she said, mischief in her voice.

"Try and stop me."

I walked over to it and sat down. It would be easy to operate when you had hands on both wheels. I had to make do with one, the one not in the sling. There was even a brake.

"Only thing it needs is a cushion for the seat."

"Maybe we could find a model made out of solid gold for you."

"Could you get one with some diamonds and rubies in it, too?"

"You want me to push you for a while, Your Majesty? There're handle grips on the back of it."

"That'd be nice. Then I can wave at my subjects."

I got to see the rest of the hospital. The first floor of it, anyway. Eight rooms, four to a side. Bright and white and clean in the autumn sunlight coming through the windows. Nurses in white, a pair of male helpers who wore street clothes and toted mops and buckets and brooms. Hospital filth was a scandal in the big cities. A good number of people died in hospitals from infections they picked up there. She explained that the surgery was on the second floor.

I was about to say that despite the fact that I enjoyed her company, I wouldn't mind getting around by myself in this chair. See what kinds of speed and turning skills I could impress myself with.

But I didn't need to. She was called to the second floor by a nurse who sounded as if she was about to give in to panic. The newspapers kept assuring us that surgical procedures were on the cusp of new breakthroughs that would save many, many more lives. Until then surgery was something of a coin toss. People spent a long time saying goodbye to their loved ones before entering surgery. And with good reason. A whole bunch of them would never see their loved ones again.

I got a good twenty minutes until my good arm gave out and I decided to roll back to my room. I parked the wheelchair next to my bed, climbed out of it and proceeded to lie down. I almost laid on top of the envelope. Nothing on the front of it. A letter inside.

*I'll be back this afternoon to see you. There are
things you should know about my husband.*

Mrs. James Andrews

Pencil. On the back of a flier advertising a sale at
the general store. I spent three minutes trying to figure out who Mrs. James Andrews might be.

When Jane came in to see how I was doing after
setting speed records in the wheelchair, I said, "Know
a Mrs. James Andrews?"

"Tib and James. James's wife. Gwen. A very nice
woman. She stopped in to talk to you, but when I
told her about the wheelchair she said not to bother
you. I told her you were having fun. She's a very nice
woman."

"I thought James was Cree. Where'd he pick up
'Andrews'?"

"The Indian agent who got James the scouting job
with the Army. His name was Andrews. James figured that when he dealt with the white world it was
easier to have a white name. So he took the James
from James Fenimore Cooper, which one of the missionaries read to James's tribe, and Andrews from the
Indian agent. She said she'd see you when you got
out of here, which I told her would be soon."

"She say what she wanted?"

She shook her pretty head. "Just that she needed to
talk to you about James. She isn't doing very well.
Understandably. They've got a little one. Luckily,
James came into some money last spring. He ordered
one of those houses you can get through the Sears
catalog. He and Tib put it up in about four days."

"How'd he come into money?"

"No idea. Maybe that's what she wants to talk to you about."

"—she's white?"

"Daughter of a missionary. James had the reputation of being a pretty rough character, but she did a lot to calm him down. Having a kid helped, too. He was a very attentive father. It's too bad he could never find any real work that paid him much. He saw that Sears ad they run in magazines for those houses you can order—and that's all he thought of, she said. He was bound and determined to build one for them. It really became an obsession. The trouble was, he couldn't figure out where he'd get the money. Then this money just came in." Then: "So how was the ride?"

"If I had both arms, I could double my speed."

She took the letter from my fingers, set it on the stand next to my bed, then pressed me back against the mattress. She pulled up the covers and said, "You'll have some food in about half an hour. See if you can take a nap. You still need to build your strength back up."

I skipped the manly protestations. It was fun to play strong man but I figured my face was blanched again from the workout with the wheelchair. A weariness had set in, too. The poison might be out of me, but my full strength hadn't returned.

I dozed off so quickly I didn't even hear her leave. Next thing I was aware of was the tray being set down on my bed stand. The smells of beef, a potato, and beets got my eyes open. This was the first real food I'd had since they'd put me in this room. Real food. I sat up.

The nurse's assistant who'd delivered the food

smiled at me. "You need any help cutting that slice of beef?"

"No," I said, "because I'll just eat it like this."

I held up the delicious-looking cut of beef and proceeded to eat it with my fingers. Right then I didn't give much of a damn about table manners.

The nurse's assistant laughed. "Good to see a man your size put the food away. Used to see my dad eat like that, God rest him."

I would have said something sentimental about her old man, but I was too busy cramming food into my face.

Chapter 6

"You're Mr. Ford."

"That I am."

"My name's Gwendolyn Andrews."

"Hello, Gwendolyn."

I judged her to be a very comely prairie-hardened thirty years old. Dark, gray-streaked hair; tanned, skinny, farm-girl body. Would be able to handle herself in most situations. Which was probably why she didn't seem intimidated at all right now.

"There are some things I'd like to tell you. We both had loved ones die. So we both want to find out the truth."

"Please pull the chair up."

Once she was seated, she used her long, tanned hands to smooth out the simple brown dress she wore. She spoke softly, purposefully, intelligently.

"I'm sorry I dragged him into it, Gwendolyn."

"You didn't drag him into it. He wanted to go. He was excited to go. So was Tib. That's why they were killed. Your brother, too."

"You're confusing me here, Gwendolyn."

"Gwen."

"All right, Gwen. My brother was killed because of the gun he was trying to sell."

"You sure of that?"

"Pretty sure."

"Well, you might be surprised. I think it was because of James."

"What's he got to do with it?"

"Somebody's been wanting to kill James for several months now. You hired Tib and James, and the man saw a way to kill him and blame it on somebody else. And he was right. Everybody thinks it was because of your brother and his gun. But it wasn't."

"You have a name for this man?"

"No. But in the past half year or so, James has been shot at twice, and once when he was sleeping alone in our new house, somebody set a rabid dog on him. James was lucky because he always slept with a gun underneath his pillow. He heard the dog snarling in the other room. He woke up in time."

I'd been lying down. I must've winced when I sat up because she said, "I should wait till you feel better."

"You can't walk out on me now. You've got a lot more to tell me and I want to hear it."

"But you made a face . . ."

"A little pain. Nothing much. I'd be most appreciative if you'd pour me some coffee out of that pot there, and I'll get a smoke going." Jane had rolled me half a dozen smokes.

Gwen touched the pot. "It's cold."

"I got used to drinking it cold in the war. Had a friend named Daniel Port who preferred it that way."

I sat up straight, struck the lucifer with my thumbnail, took a nice, deep drag, and then said, "So why don't you fill in everything for me. I got in at the end of this thing."

She hesitated, the large, savvy, brown eyes reflecting sorrow. "A lot of this will make me feel as if I'm dishonoring my husband's memory. But I want to find out what really happened out there at your brother's ranch."

I let her take her time. And finally she spoke.

Gwen's story went this way: David Ford, my brother, hired James to be a kind of night watchman. This was right after David moved here and began refining the gun he'd stolen. David was impressed by how James presented himself.

What David didn't know, but a lot of townspeople did, was that James usually found a way to double his money no matter what kind of job he took. If you hired him to move furniture for you, you had to be careful that he didn't steal something from your house while he was in there. If he worked in your stable for a month, you often found that one or two of your horses had been rustled. If you hired him to work on your farm, you could just about bet that he'd swipe as much produce as he could, and then hide it along the edge of your property so that he could sneak back at night and get it. He was the same with his own people. He stole from them every chance he got, which was why Indians didn't trust him any more than white people did. But he was such a hard and careful worker that folks put up with his indiscretions.

He was the same way with secrets. James knew a

lot of secrets. It was joked that, in fact, James knew more secrets than God. This was because you could never be sure where he was at any given moment. People had found him in their barns, closets, wagons, trees, root cellars. He never seemed to bother people. He just, he explained, liked to hear things. It was for this reason that certain people in town liked to bestow "favors" on him, usually in the form of money. A cynic might call this money blackmail. James preferred the term favors. It sounded a lot friendlier. He knew that he should never demand too much, because that would just lead to trouble. But he'd kind of sidle up to you and whisper a few sentences about what he'd overheard you say, and then soon enough you'd be giving him monthly "favors" like some of your friends.

He might hear you say something about the lady you saw on the side, or he might hear you say something about how you were cheating your business partner, or he might hear you say something about the arson fire you set because you were in dire need of insurance cash.

Tib, Gwen said, was fascinated by James. The way Gwen explained it, Tib had always wanted to be a rogue like the ones you read about in dime novels. Men who dazzled rich, beautiful women with their charms and then later broke into fancy boudoirs to steal jewels and diamonds. The trouble was, Tib was your basic plow jockey who didn't have the pluck or the imagination it took to steal a stick of licorice from Mr. Adler's candy counter over to the general store.

So he sort of lived through James. James was better than reading a book, according to Tib. Every day of the week, James would do something—never anything big, except for the occasional horse stealing, because he didn't want to go to prison—but something interesting.

The one thing she resented about James was that he had secrets he wouldn't share with her. Even when she begged him sometimes he wouldn't tell her. He always said that if anything bad happened, she wouldn't be involved in any way.

One night, several months back, James got drunk and did tell her that he'd learned something important out to David Ford's ranch. That's all he would say. Soon after that he came into a lot of money. A lot by their standards, anyway. They bought the Sears house and put it up. This took all their money. James had to work as hard as ever to support them.

But it was about that time that somebody tried to kill him. Once, twice, three times. For the first time ever, she saw her husband afraid. But he wouldn't tell her anything more than he had that one drunken night.

Then the trouble at David's ranch, and James, Tib, and David were dead.

"Everybody thinks this was about the gun, but I'm not sure it was."

The good ones take every path pointed out to them. I'm talking here about any kind of investigative man or woman you care to name. Unless it involves ghosties or goblins or spheres in the sky (all of which you hear about more frequently than you might imagine), the good investigator follows every path pointed out to him. He does not, however, always hold out much hope that he'll find much on any given path.

You have a man, my own brother, with an experimental weapon much sought around the world. You have four men of varying reputations trying to possess that gun. There is a shootout. Brother is killed. Gun vanishes.

One of the men who died in the shootout came into some unexpected money a few months back. Tempting to think that this might have some bearing on the shootout. But here you have a man, James, who by all accounts was a thief and likely a blackmailer. There could be many other explanations than the gun as to how he came into the windfall.

But, if you're good, you don't dismiss it. Because there's just enough of a vague connection to making traveling that path worthwhile—if you are a serious investigator.

"How about this?" I said. "How about if I check out what I think happened and at the same time check out what you think happened?"

"You'd really do that?"

"Sure. Why not?"

"Well, James—a Cree."

"He died helping me. I owe him that much, at least."

She took my hand. She was, as I'd guessed, strong and vital. The grip confirmed that. You take a pioneer woman, this being a theory I've had for years, and put her up against your average city man in a fight—and it's likely the pioneer woman will win. Fourteen-, fifteen-hour days of the kind of hard labor you rarely get even in most prisons—she may be slim, she may look feminine as hell when she's gussied up for a barn dance, but underestimate her at your peril.

Then she was kissing me on the forehead and saying, "Thank you so much. I just want to learn the truth."

"So do I."

She turned and walked out of the room. For a moment my eyes watched her slender, but very female, backside. But then my gaze drifted up to the wheelchair. I wanted to see if I could improve on my top speed.

But first . . . a nap.

Chapter 7

Two days later, I left the hospital. My gun arm remained in the sling, my knees trembled sometimes, and I had a vague headache.

I put on a pretty good show for the townspeople who saw me make my uncertain way down the hospital steps and onto the sidewalk. A few people walked very wide of me, as if whatever I had just might be contagious. A few of them politely stepped aside to let me dodder my way past them. The hospital had urged me to let one of their people accompany me. But pride wouldn't let me. Who the hell couldn't survive a minor gunshot wound? Apparently, I couldn't, not with any stamina or grace, anyway. I stumbled once, falling to my knee as if I were proposing marriage to a ravishing ghost woman nobody but I could see. Another time, drained, I fell against a hitching rack and stayed there for a good three or four minutes. But finally, and for no reason I could figure out, I got some serious strength back. I didn't wobble nearly as much, the cloudiness of my vision cleared up, and I even managed to get a few smiles from passing pretty women as I doffed my hat.

The first thing I did was go to the café where I'd had the good steak the other night. I ate a slab of meat as close to raw as I could get without making the cook sick. I'm a believer in the curative powers of animal blood.

The serving woman started smiling at me as I kept asking her for more bread and then a few more potatoes and then just a wee bit more beef. She was ahead of me in the dessert department. She brought forth a slice of chocolate cake that had to exhaust her just to carry. She set it down in front of me, along with a clean fork, and watched me begin to attack that cake with a passion I usually saved for the bedroom.

She laughed. "You been lost in the mountains, have you?"

"Pretty close. Lost in a hospital."

"Well, you're makin' up for lost time today."

The second thing I did was stop in a store and buy myself a shirt. I traveled with three. But the one with the bullet holes needed replacing. The clerk said that I should try and buy a shirt that went with my sling, but I said that that didn't matter to me. I hoped to have the shirt a whole lot longer than I had the sling.

"You have some kind of hunting accident, did you?" he said. "I mean that's a gunshot wound, isn't it?"

Wasn't any of his damned business. "Bear."

"Bear?"

"Uh-huh. Took a big bite out of my shoulder."

"My Lord, that musta hurt."

"Well, it did a little bit. But the bear was worse off than I was."

"You shoot him, did you?" He was eager for the whole story.

"Nope. Bit him right back. Right on the same spot on his shoulder that he bit me on mine." I smiled big and wide and crazy. You know how bullshitters smile. "I guess I surprised him so much he just skedaddled out of the camp I'd made and never bothered me again."

The clerk didn't have much to say after that. He wrote up my order and seemed mighty relieved when I left. Maybe he was afraid I'd take a big bite out of his shoulder.

The third thing I did was go back to my hotel. Not to my room, but to the front. I wanted to know which rooms Dennis Wayland and Lee Spenser were staying in. It was convenient that two of the men on the list were staying in my hotel.

The clerk gave me the room numbers, then said, "But they're not in their rooms. They're in having coffee." He nodded a shining, bald head in the direction of the hotel restaurant. "Those slings are a nuisance, aren't they? I had to wear one for a month one time. And wait till you take it off. You won't have any real feeling in your arm for a day or two."

I thanked him with a nod and then went into the restaurant. It was Victorian in the heaviness of its furnishings and the lack of sunlight. There was an almost funereal sense to the large room. All the workers wore clothes of dark brown and black. Cheery.

Wayland and Spenser made it easy for me. They were the only two people in the place except for a thin woman with twitching nervous eyes, sipping tea.

Wayland and Spenser both watched me walk toward them. When I was about halfway there they glanced at each other.

I moved the discussion along right away. I set my

inspector's badge down and pulled out a chair with my good hand and sat down.

The heavy red-haired man in the dark suit said, "You must be working with the marshal."

"Are you Wayland?" I asked him.

"No. Spenser." There was something of the Viking about him. Maybe it was the red hair and the broken nose. Or maybe it was the simple, deep-blue ferocity of the pitiless eyes. "You'd think the government would have better ways of wasting money than to have people like you follow us around." His size and attitude suggested strength.

"I'm Wayland, Mr. Ford."

"We need to talk a little bit," I said.

"I'm trying to have a goddamn drink and a goddamn meal if you don't goddamn mind it," Spenser said.

They make a mistake, men like these two. They work for the rich and powerful and then slowly begin to believe that they're rich and powerful themselves. They're not. They're hired functionaries, the same as I am.

"Mind telling me why you're in town?" I said.

"None of your damned business," Spenser snapped.

"Oh, hell, don't let him rile you, Spenser," Wayland said. He was tall, slim, lawyerly, right down to the way he tucked his thumbs into the slant pockets of his vest. He had thinning brown hair and shrewd brown eyes. "He thinks he matters because he has a badge, and that's supposed to frighten people like us."

Wayland talked like a lawyer, too, but there was a hurt, weak, quality to his eyes, and his voice was pitched higher than he probably liked.

But Spenser couldn't let go. "Some gunny with a badge thinks he's some big important man." He glared up at me. He had a bubble of steak sauce hanging off his fierce red mustache. This probably wasn't a good time to mention it. "There's nothing illegal in what I'm doing. I work for the Brits, yes. The Brits are friends of ours, in case you hadn't heard. And they need to defend themselves the same way we do. That means keeping up with new weapons. I'm here by invitation of . . ." He hadn't made the connection before. "Ford. I was here at David Ford's invitation." His rage cooled some. "Was he a relative?"

"Brother."

The two men looked at each other again.

Wayland said, "That's odd, isn't it? You investigating your own brother?"

They obviously didn't know that I'd used the gun as a pretext. Yes, the government wanted it. That had been their interest in David. Mine was in saving my brother's life. If another investigator had been sent, he likely would have killed David on the spot.

"I grew up with him," I said. "I knew his patterns and how he thought. It made sense for the Army to send me down here."

"This hayseed marshal seems to think one of us killed him and took the gun," Spenser said.

"Why just one of you?" I said. "What if two of you got together? Or three or four?"

"Bad theory," Wayland said. "We each represent a different party. We couldn't work together." He'd eaten little. He'd left most of a steak on his plate, potatoes and applesauce untouched.

"Which party is it that you represent, Mr. Wayland?"

"I'm afraid that's none of your business."

"I wouldn't say that, I'm afraid."

"Oh?"

"If I find out that you're representing a hostile government, then I can have you held until some other Federal boys get down here to ask you some questions."

"If you think you scare us, you're wrong," Spenser said. "You shouldn't try and intimidate anybody when you've got your arm in a sling."

His right hand was resting flat on the pure-white tablecloth. I grabbed it with my left hand and squeezed it so tight I could feel the bones grinding against each other. His size and his cold stern face didn't help him much. He was all pain, helpless as hell right now.

"You sonofabitch," he said when I let go his wide, long hand.

"I just wanted to make sure you didn't confuse me with some sort of invalid," I said. "Because I'm not."

As he rubbed his damaged hand, he glared at me.

"Neither of us killed your brother," Wayland said.

"I suppose you can prove that?"

Spenser stood up. "I need to relieve myself, gentlemen. If you'd be so kind as to explain to this cretin about our alibi, Mr. Wayland, I'd be most grateful."

I didn't see the jerking limp or the heavily built-up shoe until he'd taken two steps. His size, but most of all his arrogance, made his limp seem impossible. He kept his head tilted so that he could watch me watch him. Instinct made me want to pity him. But he didn't want my pity and he made sure he didn't get it. "Don't worry, Ford. Even with this foot, I'm twice the man you'll ever be."

Wayland sipped coffee. "You didn't make any friends here, I'll tell you that."

"What makes you think I'd want you two as friends, Wayland? You sell arms to the highest bidder."

"We have alliances. We represent our clients' best interests."

"Unless some other 'client' offers you more money."

He leaned back and looked at me, his eyes dark in the shadowy restaurant. I wanted to be outside. Away from the gloom. Away from these two. There were a lot of filthy ways to make money, but selling arms had to be one of the filthiest. "If one of us had killed your brother and taken the gun, the first thing we'd have done is get the hell out of here before the marshal could stop us."

"That's the last thing you would've done. If you'd killed him and taken the gun, you would have had to stay here. Leaving would make you look guilty for sure."

"We were here before," he said. "This is the second time your brother invited us. We had a good relationship with him."

This was something I hadn't known. Nobody'd mentioned it before. "When were you here?"

"Seven months ago. All four of us. Your brother wanted to whet our appetites. The gun still needed work, but it was well enough along that we could get a sense of its power. We saw it and we went back to our respective clients and told them about it. They then began figuring out what they were going to bid for the project. All the clients wanted to have a guarantee that it was an exclusive. Your brother promised he could deliver sixty of them three months after the demonstration he gave us the day he died."

"He wasn't set up for manufacturing."

"He didn't have to be. There was a firm back East."

"So you gave him sealed bids?"

"Of course. He couldn't afford to alienate us, so he acted honestly. Your brother was a very energetic man. He always had something to sell. Everything from guns to information. So he always took sealed bids and opened them in front of everybody placing bids. The highest bidder won. Simple as that."

"Maybe one of you got greedy."

"We didn't bring money, only the bids."

"Of course. But you could tell your client that somebody else had the gun now and you needed to pay him."

He smiled. "You have a devious mind, Mr. Ford. You could be one of us."

Spenser came back. As he sat down, Wayland said, "I was just telling Mr. Ford that he was devious enough to be one of us."

"He's too stupid to be one of us."

"If I didn't know better," Wayland said, "I'd say you two didn't like each other."

"You never did get around to telling me about your alibi, Wayland."

Spenser snapped, "Then *I'll* tell you. There's a whorehouse on Dodge Street. 33 is the address. The four of us rented it for the night. Middle of the week business is slow there. They gave us a special rate. We did everything you might expect."

Wayland: "I dimly recall doing a few things I hadn't expected."

"That's your alibi? A madam?"

"Tell me, Ford," Spenser said, his entire body tense with anger at my simple presence in his world. "Do you only deal with people of high moral character?"

"Obviously not. I'm sitting here with you two, aren't I?"

Wayland laughed. "I have to admit, that's a good one."

"He's an asshole."

"Oh, c'mon, Spenser. We're probably just as bad as he says we are. We do sell to the highest bidder and sometimes they aren't exactly virgins."

"You're agreeing with him?" Spenser snapped. "We work in a capitalist society. This bastard sounds like an anarchist." He turned his angry gaze on me. "And anyway, I wonder if he has any idea how many people in the Department of the Army we've bribed over the years. You've probably taken a little graft yourself, Ford, you sanctimonious prick."

"Shout a little louder, Spenser, she wasn't able to pick that last one up." I nodded to the prim lady sipping tea several tables away. "Repeat the part about how you bribed people in the Department of the Army. I'll need a witness to get a warrant for your arrest."

"Arrest?" Wayland said. "We were just having a little fun here . . ."

"Spenser here just admitted to a federal crime. The department's well aware that some of its employees take bribes for information. We're gradually getting rid of them. And once we do, we'll start on people like our friend Spenser here."

"You're no friend of mine," Spenser said. "Don't even joke about it."

It was time to leave. "I'll no doubt want to talk to you again."

"Fair warning?" Wayland smirked.

"Something like that, I suppose. In the meantime, tell Spenser here that he needs to relax a little. For the sake of his heart. Unless he killed my brother. Then he won't have to worry about his heart. I'll take care of that for him."

Wayland still seemed amused by it all. Maybe he just liked to see a good fight. "I'd watch out for this fellow if I were you, Spenser."

I decided to end all the fun. "The same goes for you, too, Wayland."

He smiled, and the smile said that not only was he smarter, richer, and prettier than I was, but he was also better at the little game we were playing.

I was glad to leave.

Chapter 8

Despite what the ministers will tell you, there are whorehouses and there are whorehouses. There are some, for instance, where you are likely to get (a) robbed, (b) diseased, (c) blackmailed. There are others where you don't want to see the girls you'll be going upstairs with because if you saw them first you wouldn't *go* upstairs. And then there are those where the girls are pretty and checked once a month by the local docs, and the bouncer, usually Negro, is there to keep peace and quiet, not to rob you.

I had the impression, as soon as I stepped inside her door, that Luellen Conroy ran the latter variety. The house was clean, the furnishings new, the air fresh smelling. Luellen herself was a trim little woman in a tan business suit, pince-nez glasses, and a quick, pleasant smile. Her graying hair was pulled back into a chignon.

She answered the door herself and said, "I'm afraid we're not open now, sir. If you'd like to come back around four, we'll be glad to see you."

I showed her my badge.

She smiled. "Well, a Federale. I'm impressed. Had a

lot of lawmen through here before, but never a Federal man. And especially not one as nice-looking as you."

Prim and proper as she was, she had to get a whorehouse compliment out. In her calling, flattery was meaningless and mandatory.

"Afraid I'm here on business."

"Business? A Federal man? Well, c'mon in."

She led me down a narrow hall. A gray tomcat waddled after us. "He may hiss at you. I've put him on a diet and he doesn't like it. He takes it out on everybody. I've got a couple of gals who are just like him. I say lose a few pounds and they act like I told them to get an arm amputated or something."

She said all this as she walked, without once looking back at me.

Her office was painted yellow, with yellow curtains and mahogany office furnishings. Clean, competent, like the lady herself.

"Like some coffee?"

"That sounds good, actually."

She had a graceful silver pot on top of a three-shelf bookcase. She poured steaming coffee into two rather dainty cups and handed me one.

"I told the girls they could sleep in. Had a little trouble last night. Couple cattlemen got pretty rowdy and started fighting with a couple of the other customers. One of them pulled a gun and held one of the girls hostage." She smiled. "He was so drunk he couldn't tell me why he was holding her hostage. I had to sit up half the night talking to him. He was a pretty sad case. Some people shouldn't drink. I didn't think he'd shoot her on purpose, but there was the chance he might accidentally misfire or something, so I had to be careful."

"You didn't send for the marshal?"

"Charley Wickham?" She smiled. "Charley makes his money the easy way. He stops by to pick up his 'stipend,' as he calls it, once a month but otherwise he wants to forget this house even exists. That doesn't make him bad, just sensible. Every lawman I've ever known takes sin money. He'd come out here if we had a murder—God forbid—but anything else, he lets us handle."

"Never samples the merchandise?"

"Nope. Never did." She sat back in her chair and picked up one of three cigarettes she'd rolled for herself. She lighted it with a stick match which she snuffed out between thumb and forefinger. "Your brother was here a few times."

"Doesn't surprise me."

"Some of the time I liked him."

"Our whole family's that way. Some of the time we're likable."

"You, too?"

"Imagine I'm the same way, yes."

"I don't think that nurse of his ever knew about it. Stuck-up gal. I send our girls to the hospital for their monthly checkups. She's never very friendly to them." She took a long drag on her cigarette. "She put your arm in that sling?"

"Matter of fact, she did."

"I could make a lot of money on her. A certain kind of man goes for a woman like that. Aloof. Makes the men think they're getting a real prize."

"You want me to mention that to her?"

She grinned. "Oh, sure. And then you'll have your other arm in a sling."

"She's a pretty decent woman, actually. Once you melt the ice."

"If you like the type." Another deep drag. The smoke was baby blue in the slanting autumn sunlight through the window. "But you're not here for small talk, are you?"

"I'm here to find out if a couple of men named Spenser and Wayland rented your whole house Tuesday night?"

"And that would be the night your brother was murdered."

"You keep up on the news."

"Half the merchants in town sneak over here. We hear all the news and all the gossip."

"So did they?"

"I can't give you the answer you want because I wasn't in town. I have a man I see over in Riverton. I was there that evening. It was my birthday. As far as I know, they were here from about eight in the evening until about four or five the next morning. Spenser had a little trouble getting excited enough to do anything until the girls gave him a bath. That got him going. They giggled about him the last time, too."

"The last time?"

"Spenser and Wayland and the other two who came to visit your brother several months back— they all ended up here one night. The girls don't mind helping men who're having a little trouble—men who're a little shy or nervous or feel they're doing something wrong. A lot of the time that's actually sweet, believe it or not, makes the men more human and they're more grateful when they finally do get all fired up. And that means tips for the gals. But what they don't like are men who blame them. Insult them.

Tell them if they were prettier or this and that—well, they blame the woman. Spenser's like that. So they don't like him much. Wayland's fine. He just wants to have a good time."

"You say you hear gossip? You hear anything about my brother's murder?"

"Nothing you haven't heard."

"You know James Andrews?"

A sour face. "Everybody knew James. And almost nobody liked him."

"Why's that?"

"He had a way of snooping around. Finding things out that people didn't want found out."

"He ever bother you?"

A deep drag on her cigarette. "Are you kidding? He used to sit up in that tree over on the corner of my property and write down the names of all the so-called respectable men who snuck in my back door. I think a few of them gave him a little money a few times, but that wasn't good for my business. I had to hire a couple boys who were passing through town— gunnies, I guess you'd say—and they gave James the kind of beating that takes a long, long time to get over. He never sat up in that tree again, I'll tell you that."

There wasn't much more to say. I wondered about Spenser and Wayland. Unless one of the girls contradicted them and said that she saw one or both of them sneak out, their alibi from eight to dawn was covered. But the doc who'd examined David's body said that he'd probably been killed in the very early part of the evening. It wouldn't have taken much to kill him just at twilight and then sneak back to town and the whorehouse.

"Ask your girls if they saw either Wayland or Spenser sneak off that night, would you?"

She ground her smoke out in a glass ashtray and stood up. I guessed our meeting was over. She came around the desk and gently touched the elbow of my good arm. "I'll make a point of asking them this afternoon."

She guided me to the front door.

"You're welcome here any time, Mr. Ford."

"I appreciate the invitation. Maybe I'll take you up on that."

"That means 'no,' doesn't it?"

I laughed. "Yep, I expect it does."

"Too proud?"

I shook her hand. She had a hell of a grip for such a small woman.

"No," I smiled, "too cheap."

"Oh, sure. I'll bet."

I spent an hour at the mortuary where they were boxing David up to be shipped back to the ancestral home down South. I hadn't had any contact with my folks in years, and didn't intend to start now. I just wanted to make sure that David looked as good as possible. My mother would appreciate that. She was awfully fussy about how people dressed. Even dead people. Or maybe especially dead people. In her crowd, looking your best included being buried.

While I was working with Mr. Harold Newcomb, who owned the mortuary, a thin, middle-aged woman in an appropriately black, high-collared dress, slammed away at typewriter keys in a small office off the room that could be rented for wakes.

Whenever Newcomb was called away, which was frequently, he told me to look over the three types of shipping boxes he sold. A couple of times when he was called away, the thin woman in black quit her typing and came quickly out of the office, heading in my direction. But each time she started to speak to me, Newcomb came back, and she pretended to be just walking through the viewing area.

I concluded my business in Newcomb's office, paying cash, with the woman pounding away on the typewriter. I got a receipt, a damp handshake, and an offer to escort me to the front door. But before I could say anything, the thin woman said, "I have to run over to the newspaper for some more letterhead, Mr. Newcomb. I can walk him outdoors."

"Fine, Beth. I appreciate that."

She grabbed a shawl and off we went.

She didn't speak until we were outside on the steps. "I'm sorry about your brother, Mr. Ford."

"Thanks."

"I don't mean that professionally. I mean, I don't say it just because I'm in the funeral business."

"I know what you mean. And thanks again."

Clamor from wagons, buggies, a stagecoach. Bright-sounding birds; merry people in the cherished sunlight. Odd to see all this life from the steps of a funeral home.

"I don't mean to speak out of turn, but there's something I wanted to tell you about because there's no other lawman around."

I'd felt that she had some message for me. "All right."

"Last year a friend of mine died. A woman named Louise. I happened to be working late when they brought her in. Mr. Newcomb is also the county medical examiner. I know what he put on the death certificate, but I don't think it was correct. I think somebody—well, you know."

The door opened. Mr. Newcomb, who did not look happy, said, "Something's come up, Miss Cave. Would you come in here, please?"

"But I need to get paper and . . ."

Unhappiness became frozen anger. "Right now, if you please, Miss Cave." Then, nodding to me, "Good day, Mr. Ford."

I was being dismissed. But I had the idea that she was facing an even sterner fate. He'd obviously overheard us talking. Obviously.

The next place I stopped was to visit Thomas Brinkley and Giles Fairbain, the other two men who'd been dealing with my brother for his new machine gun. They were staying at the Excelsior Hotel, which was a bit finer than where I was staying. The halls had been waxed and smelled of sweet polish. The maids scurried rather than walked, and smiled rather than merely nodded.

Neither man was in, as the rather disapproving gent behind the desk told me after grudgingly giving me their room numbers. Apparently, my sling displeased him. Must've given him the impression that I was some sort of ruffian—that was the prissy word his kind would use—and therefore not the sort of man one would expect to stay at such a refined hotel as this. Too bad I didn't have some fresh horse shit on my boots. I could have given his Persian rug a little more color of the brown variety.

I walked over to the marshal's office. Clarion was clearing off the front desk for the day. Most of the items went into the wastebasket. "You looking for the marshal?"

"Yep. He in?"

"Anything I can help you with? He's pretty busy with paperwork."

"Why don't I just walk back there?"

He said, "Believe it or not, we have a system here."

It wasn't worth pushing. He was doing his job. "Ask him if he'll see me." We stared at each other a long moment.

"I'll be right back," he said. He walked back and spoke to the marshal in a low voice.

Clarion came back and said, "The marshal said c'mon back."

I walked back. Wickham's door was open. He sat behind his desk, staring at a small photograph. I couldn't see the side with the chemical on it, the side with the actual picture, but even so he hurriedly got rid of it. Opened the middle drawer of his desk, dropped the photograph in, slid the door shut.

"Well, if it isn't Mr. Ford."

He nodded to the chair in front of his desk. "Sittin's free this time of day."

"Who could turn down an offer like that?"

He leaned back in his squeaky desk chair, folded his

hands over his stomach. "I'll bet I know why you're here."

"You a mind reader, are you?"

"Nope. A snoop is what I am. Well, not personally. But my men are. And one of them told me James's wife came to see you in the hospital."

"That right?"

His chair squawked when he leaned back. "I imagine she told you the same story she told me."

"You want to go first?"

"Don't bother me none. She doesn't think that your brother and her husband and Tib died because of that gun. She thinks James was blackmailing somebody."

"And you don't believe that?"

"You mean was he blackmailing somebody? Hell, yes. But he was never into big money. Just enough to keep food on the table."

"Where'd he get the money for the new house?"

"Maybe he saved his money. Maybe he got lucky one time. But if he was blackmailing somebody that important around here it would've had to involve some kind of crime. And if it involved some kind of crime, I would've heard about it by now."

"When's the last murder you had here before my brother?"

"Over a year ago."

"Rapes? Major robberies?"

"About the same."

"Why would the blackmail have to be local?"

"James rarely left town. All the people he blackmailed were local."

There wasn't much left to cross swords over.

"Besides, the gun's gone, Ford. Whoever did the

killing took the gun. And whoever took the gun would have to be somebody who knew how to unload a piece of stolen merchandise that a whole bunch of powerful people were looking for."

"Meaning one of the four men who came here to see my brother David?"

"Can you figure it any other way?"

I started to say that, no, I couldn't. Mrs. Andrews's story hadn't struck me as particularly sound to begin with. Now it sounded even less so.

I was about to say that when Frank knocked on the door. "Curly Holmes fell off the wagon again and he's shootin' up his house. His wife's afraid he'll shoot out all their windows again. Says she can't afford to buy new ones. Says she don't want me to go with her 'cause Curly gets mad every time he sees me. So she wants you to go with her."

Suddenly, with gunshot clarity, a woman began sobbing in the outer office.

"That fuckin' Curly," Marshal Wickham said, standing up. "I guess you'll have to excuse me, Ford."

We shook hands briefly. I went out the back door. I never know what to do around weeping women.

The hotel clerk remembered me from earlier in the day.

"Mr. Fairbain and Mr. Brinkley came in about an hour ago. But you might like to wet your whistle first. In fact, I think you may find Mr. Brinkley in there now."

Helpful fellow. Managed to hook me up with the two men I wanted to see and shill for the hotel's saloon at the same time.

"I've never met him," I said. "You happen to remember what he's wearing?"

The clerk leaned forward, glanced around and then tapped his cheek. "Small birthmark on his right cheek. You'll see it right away."

The saloon strove hard for dignity. The two men behind the bar had slicked-down hair, fancy mustaches, and starched white shirts with snappy red arm garters. The clientele looked to be free of ruffians: mostly businessmen, local and passing through. The serving woman was older and therefore not the kind to get pinched. And the bug-eyed man on the high stool in the corner used his fiddle to soothe rather than excite. In other words, the place looked boring as hell.

Only one man bore a birthmark on his cheek. He looked New England rather than Western. One of those stern, thin-lipped men who disapproved of just about everything that passed in front of him.

"Mr. Brinkley?"

He sat by himself, tucked into a corner beneath a small painting of an elegant ballet dancer with a pretty, wan face.

He just stared at me. No hello.

"The name's Noah Ford, Mr. Brinkley."

"I was afraid of that." His celluloid collar looked sharp enough to be a weapon.

I smiled. "They warned you about me."

No offer to sit down.

"I didn't care for your brother. You won't get any sympathy here."

"I don't want any sympathy, Mr. Brinkley. I just want to know where you were the night he was murdered."

Uninvited, I sat down.

"I'm not in the habit of murdering people, if that's what you mean." He still showed signs of youthful acne, though he had to be fifty. There was a dead quality to the gray eyes that could scare the hell out of kids on a Halloween night.

"That doesn't answer my question."

"I don't intend to answer your question. It's ridiculous."

The serving woman came. I ordered coffee.

"I'd prefer it if you'd drink that somewhere else."

"Well, I'd prefer it if you'd tell me where you were the night my brother was murdered."

"There weren't many people who liked him."

"I'll bet there aren't a whole lot of people who like you, either, Mr. Brinkley. I don't know why, but I kind of have that feeling."

The dead, gray eyes were on me full force now. Not anger; disapproval. "I might as well tell you, we had an argument that afternoon. He went back on his word and I didn't like it."

"His word about what?"

Skeletal fingers wrapped around his schooner. "He told me that if I gave him a thousand dollars—a bribe—he'd let me know what the other bids were in advance."

"I thought they were sealed bids. How could he know in advance?"

He smiled with tobacco-stained teeth. It wasn't pretty. "You mustn't have known your brother very well."

"We had a difference of opinion about the war." I couldn't resist: "But then as a leading Copperhead, you must know all about that."

"The South had a right to make its own rules."

"I'm not here to argue the war. I'm just saying that you went against your own government and so did I. That gives us something in common, I guess."

"Yes, your brother said you were a spy for the North. I wouldn't be proud of that. And I resent your saying that we have anything in common. I'm a man of principle." He took a long drink of beer. I realized that the birthmark was below a crusted area of acne. He was an ugly man, and you could almost feel sorry for him if the ugliness hadn't extended to his soul.

I leaned back and sighed. "He cheated you. He pulled a very old trick on all four of you. He told each of you that if you'd give him a thousand dollars, he'd tip you to the other bids. So he pockets four thousand dollars the easy way and then sells to the highest bidder, anyway."

"He was a despicable man, your brother."

My sudden anger surprised me as much as it did him. I reached over and grabbed him by his greasy hair and lifted him off his chair. I knocked over his beer in the process. The beer ran off the edges of the table. The serving woman hurried over. People began to watch. I shoved him back in his chair.

"Whatever he was, whatever I am, he was my brother. So keep your tongue off him. He wasn't perfect and neither am I. And neither are you, Brinkley. You're an arms dealer, which isn't exactly a higher calling in my book."

I forced myself to calm down—long intakes of breath.

Brinkley gathered himself with a kind of funereal dignity, planted his gaze on the front door so that he would have no eye contact with anybody, and proceeded to leave the saloon.

I was frozen in place for a while. Everybody staring at me, everybody speculating on what had happened. Embarrassing now that the fury had quieted in me. The nice thing about rage is that nothing embarrasses you. Then comes the aftermath when you begin to second-guess yourself. Maybe I didn't have to get quite so mad . . . There were times when somebody else took over my mind. Somebody who sounded like me and thought like me, at least for the most part, but somebody who . . . There were times I didn't like to remember or think about.

I waited till their attention went back to whatever they'd been talking about before. Then I got up and walked out just the way Brinkley had. No eye contact with the drinkers who'd had a few minutes of minor violence and major thrill. And they hadn't even had to buy tickets to see it.

I remembered that Fairbain's room number was 204. I nodded to the clerk, who was apparently still innocent of the little scene I'd caused in the saloon, and went on up the stairs, passing a couple of drummers and a pair of old men who wore some kind of red lodge caps I'd never seen before. Until I found a lodge that regularly served free women, I was not about to join up.

A narrow strip of new carpeting ran down the center of the hall. The flooring was some kind of blond wood, which seemed an odd choice for a hotel, with all the shoe marks, carpetbags being dropped, and winter mud. Not to mention spills and the occasional vomit-spewing drunk. But that was their problem.

I knocked on 204 twice before I saw it, and I probably wouldn't have seen it then if the smell hadn't stung my nostrils. There are some folks who'll tell you that it doesn't smell at all. These are people, take my word for it, who've never been around it much. To me it's the stench of wet metal. That's as close as I can come to a physical description of it. A somewhat tart smell.

I walked down the hallway.

I didn't knock on Brinkley's door. We'd do a little dance, and I was in no mood for a little dance. I'd tell him who it was, and he'd say go away, and I'd say I needed to talk to him, that this was urgent, and he'd still say go away, and so I'd end up using my burglar's pick anyway. So what the hell. I used the pick, swung the door inward, and went for my gun before he could even drop the newspaper he was reading.

I didn't want to take the chance of him having a Colt lying on his belly behind the newspaper.

"Get up."

"You could be arrested for breaking in here like this." He sat on the bed with his back to the wall. His suit coat and celluloid collar were off, as was his cravat. His right white sock had a hole. His big toe peeked through. He had a violently discolored toenail. Some kind of fungus.

"I said to get up. If you don't, I'll drag you."

"What the hell's going on?"

I didn't tell him. I left the room. He followed in his stocking feet and caught up with me. When we reached the door, I said, "Watch where you step."

When he saw what I was talking about, he said, "My Lord. That's blood. From under the door."

"Sure is."

"Is he dead?"

"I don't know. I haven't been in his room. I knocked but there was no answer. So I thought we'd find out together." I gave him my best harsh laugh. "Unless you killed him. Then I guess you'd know what we're going to find, wouldn't you?"

I used the pick again and we went into the room.

PART TWO

Chapter 9

Fifteen minutes later it got awfully crowded in Fairbain's little room. Two heavyset men with a stretcher came up and took Fairbain to the hospital. They weren't the gentlest of fellows. One of them banged the center of the stretcher against the door as they were going out. The scrawny doc with one brown glass eye rolled the good one and said, "He'll live, unless you two boys kill him on the way over."

The thing with head and face wounds is that you can bleed a whole hell of a lot without being mortally wounded. Whoever had worked Fairbain over had worked him over with a sap of some kind, mistakenly assumed that he was dead, and then left. Fairbain had other ideas. He'd managed to walk or crawl across the room to the door. Unfortunately, he'd collapsed before he could get it open; collapsed in such a way that the blood from his head wounds drained between the bottom of the door and the floor.

Given the blood, I'd assumed that he'd had his throat cut, the way my brother had. The use of the sap, though, made more sense in this circumstance. No matter how deft you are with a knife, there's a fair chance the victim will have time to scream at least once before your blade opens up his throat. But if you surprise him with a sap—you can render him unconscious before he can say a word, and then ease him to the bed or the floor where you can continue to work him over quietly.

You don't want anybody screaming in a respectable hotel at the dinner hour, not unless you want to attract a lot of attention.

"What's going on here?" Marshal Charley Wickham said after the room started emptying out.

"Looks like somebody tried to kill him."

"That wouldn't be you, would it, Mr. Ford?"

I shrugged. "I don't like arms dealers, but I didn't kill this one."

Wickham regarded me thoughtfully for a minute, then went over to the closet door.

"Man hides in here. Waits for Fairbain. Fairbain opens the closet door. Man hits him so hard, Fairbain's out. Then the man goes to work on him."

"Sounds reasonable."

Wickham turned back to me. "Or somebody knocks on the door. Fairbain knows him. Fairbain opens up, man saps him, knocks him out, drags him back inside the room and goes to work on him."

"That also sounds reasonable."

"I'm not finished yet."

"Be my guest."

"Man thinks Fairbain's dead. Leaves hotel believing his work's done." Then: "Or."

"I knew there'd be an 'or.'"

"And this is pure speculation, I'm not saying it happened this way."

"Of course not."

"But just for the sake of argument, say it was you who attacked Fairbain and thought he was dead."

"Just for the sake of argument."

"You know what you'd do if you were smart, and you are smart, Ford, that's obvious to everybody."

"If I was smart—and again, just for the sake of argument since we both know I'm innocent—if I was smart, I'd go down the hall and get Brinkley and tell him that I hadn't been in Fairbain's room but that I suspected something was wrong."

"Took the words right out of my mouth."

"And you know what, Wickham? That sounds reasonable, too. Everything you've said sounds reasonable. Except I didn't try to kill him. As he'll tell you when he's conscious again."

"You know what the doc said. He said no guarantees. Fairbain might not ever recover."

A gentle knock on the half-opened door. The desk clerk. "Marshal, you asked me to round up everybody who was in his room for the past hour or so. I've got them all in 212, at the west end of the hall."

"Thanks. I appreciate it."

The desk clerk went away.

"You're thorough, Wickham."

"I'm glad you approve. A Federal man like you coming out to a Podunk town like this one and handing out compliments, wait'll I tell my deputies. They'll be proud of me."

"Especially that nephew of yours." I walked over to the door. "I'm told that a professional lawman always hires his relatives. Sure sign of somebody who knows what he's doing."

A reluctant smile. "You know, Ford, if I didn't

know better, I'd say that you don't care for me any more than I care for you."

"Oh, now, Marshal, I don't know where you'd get an idea like that."

I left, making sure to step around the blood that had yet to be wiped up.

I went down to the hotel saloon for some coffee. New customers had replaced the ones who'd watched me and Brinkley argue. Even the barmen had changed shifts. I took my coffee to a corner table and sat down.

Sipped my coffee. One thing Wickham hadn't mentioned was the gun that I felt was obviously involved in my brother's murder. And it was also likely involved in the assault on Fairbain. Attempted murder on Fairbain, actually.

Or was it? If my brother had been killed for the weapon, then hadn't his killer taken the weapon with him when he left the barn that night? And if he had the weapon, why had he gone after Fairbain?

What if David had been killed by one person and Fairbain attacked by another? That would mean that something else was going on here in addition to the hunt for the weapon.

The place started getting noisy about half an hour later. I still had the remnants of my first coffee. The serving woman had twice asked me if I'd like more. I'd said no. They obviously wanted somebody in my chair who was planning on spending some money. I didn't blame them.

I was just getting up, ready to leave, when I saw

Deputy Frank Clarion and another man walking toward me.

Clarion did a lot of waving and nodding and smiling before he got within handshaking distance of me.

"Evening, Ford. Mind if we take your table?"

"It's all yours."

"How's the shoulder?" He nodded at my sling.

"Feeling a little better, thanks."

He introduced his friend and then I left.

The temperature outdoors was probably near fifty degrees. Bonfires burned in the streets. Jack-o'-lanterns grinned ghoulishly at me in front windows. Dogs and cats made their stealthy way through the night. I must have walked for better than half an hour. A few glimpses of families gathered together in parlors made me feel lonely and sorry for myself. Every once in a while I wondered if this was any sort of life, mine. The hell of it was I hadn't known any other sort. Nothing to compare it to.

By the time I got back to the business area, I was hungry.

I walked into the café where I'd had breakfast. Jane Churchill was sitting at a table by herself. She wore a simple, blue dress that flattered her far more than her nurse's uniform did. I walked over and said hello.

Jane said, "You could always sit down, Noah."

I looked at the dinners scrawled on the blackboard.

I ordered Swiss steak and a boiled potato and

beets, and then started working on the coffee that had just been set before me.

Jane said, "Are you getting used to your sling?"

"Sort of."

"Are you in a lot of pain?"

"I try not to notice it."

She smiled. "Brave?"

"Hardly. Just practical. If you keep thinking about your pain, you have pain. If you keep busy, you don't notice it much."

"I suppose that makes sense." Then: "Oh, I found an old photograph of David this afternoon."

This time the smile was wide and deep. Fondness chased the tired look from her eyes; she looked young and sweet there in the soft lamplight of the café. "He was right out of a storybook. Nobody had ever romanced me the way he had. He was so courtly—and so much fun. That's what I couldn't resist about him. His charm and how he liked to play at things. A part of him never grew up and I loved that. Sometimes I wanted him to be more mature and responsible—sometimes I got pretty mad at him—but the good times made up for all that."

It made me jealous, hearing this kind of tribute. Not jealous of her or David in particular, but of any two people who could have a relationship like that. The even stranger thing was that eventually I'd suffocate in the setup she'd described. The fun would go gray; the nights would pall. But I'd never had a relationship like that and it was probably something I should try at least once before a bullet or time itself started making my tombstone.

Then she said, "Fairbain was hurt tonight or something?"

"Somebody tried to kill him."

"You said 'tried.' "

"He's at your hospital. I'm wondering if it had anything to do with David and the gun."

"You think it doesn't?"

"What did David think of Fairbain?"

"He didn't like him. He didn't like any of them, in fact. The gun merchants. They were like spoiled children. They were always threatening him."

"Threatening him with what?"

"Oh, you know how men talk. Fairbain said that if David didn't sell him the gun, he could always hire somebody to steal it from David. The others were always threatening to expose him to the government. Or to put the word out that the weapons David had didn't really work the way David claimed. Or that maybe they'd figured out how the gun functioned and they could get somebody to make a copy of the weapon for them and save themselves a lot of money."

"David didn't believe it?"

"Of course not. I mean, it was obvious they knew that David had what they wanted, and that they were going to pay a lot of money for it. The only thing he was afraid of was that a gang would come in the middle of the night and steal it. He hid it somewhere. Even I didn't know where it was."

"He didn't trust you?"

"He didn't want to see me get tortured. So he didn't tell me. Wherever it was, he'd set up a trap with nitroglycerin. If you went near the weapon, the nitro would explode and kill you. You had to know how to undo the trigger mechanism he'd set up. David told me he'd used a similar setup when he'd been in Cincinnati and that it blew up a man so badly that he was just pieces of meat after the blast. And the gun was fine."

"Then maybe it really wasn't for the gun."

"What wasn't?"

I thought a long moment. My food had been brought to me and was setting there getting cold. "David's murder."

"Why do you say that?"

"I'm assuming that David told all his potential customers about the nitro."

"Of course. Fair warning."

"Then they'd know better than to try and steal it. Unless they hired a nitro man who knew how to disarm the nitro trigger."

We finished our coffee. I paid the bill. We went outside and walked.

"I wish it stayed fall forever," she said. "David always said that it was his favorite season, too. He said he used to hide up in the treehouse and scare you."

"Yeah. He loved Halloween when we were little. And he'd have lived in trees if my folks had let him."

"He must've been so cute when he was young. He made such a good-looking man."

"He was lucky to have an admirer like you."

"Much more than an admirer. I loved him, Noah."

This was the second time today I'd felt pretty isolated. I suppose David's death had gotten to me more than I'd thought at first. Whatever our differences, I'd loved him, even if I hadn't liked him much. He was blood. But even more was the sense of being alone. There was no way I could ever return home. For a few years after the war I'd thought that maybe David and I could find each other and become cautious friends again. But selling arms to anybody who had the money wasn't exactly my idea of an honorable calling. He was still the old cynical David. Fun counted for more than anything else. And if it was reckless fun, fun that even destroyed lives, he didn't care.

I glanced at Jane several times as we walked along in the starlight, an occasional wagon or rider passing us by. She was making me recall how jealous I'd been of David growing up. I'd always been the good one. Took school seriously, never got into any really bad trouble, tried to show my folks how appreciative I was of all they'd given me, even though the books I'd been reading had convinced me that slavery was wrong in every respect—meaning that my father's plantation didn't have any right to exist, that the entire South had been established on the backs of slaves and was therefore corrupt. Not everybody in it, of course. Rich whites exploited and used poor whites to their own ends. David and I used to argue about this to the point of bloody noses and even a busted nose—his. He was handsomer, cleverer, slicker, but I was tougher. The temper I had couldn't be controlled past a certain point, as David had found out many times.

The mystery to me was that all the girls who tried so hard to be respectable—the daughters of other plantations—seemed drawn to David the more he got into trouble. He once had to spend a night in jail for stealing a buckboard—and some of the prettiest girls in the county were there to greet him when my father's lawyer got him released on bail.

Same way with Jane. She was the good woman every man wanted—quiet, proper, intelligent, dutiful—

and yet she'd fallen in love with a man in one of the dirtiest callings you could be in. I didn't blame David for taking up with her. I just blamed her for not seeing that sooner rather than later he'd go on to the next one.

"Well," she said, "here's my little house."

Maybe it was the moonlight. Maybe it was the aromas of the autumn night. Maybe it was just her pretty face. Whatever it was, the house, which was really just a cottage, seemed like something out of a painting, with its thatched roof and mullioned windows. A swift, high creek ran behind it, starlit birch trees like silver sentries along the edge of the water. There was even a sweet, plump mama raccoon crouched in the long grass with her young ones. Mama's eyes glistened and gleamed the way only a raccoon's can.

"This is quite a place," I said.

"Really? Everybody tells me how small it is."

There was even smoke twisting up from the chimney.

"If you're here long enough, I'll make dinner for you some night."

"I'd appreciate that."

She glanced at the door with a clear longing in her eyes. "Even David consented to have dinner here a few times. He didn't like the place very much. I think he thought it was a bit 'common.' He always said that was the hardest adjustment your folks had to make—that they'd had to sell off most of the plantation and live like they were 'common.'"

I laughed. "That sounds like David. My folks have been reduced to having only one palatial estate, rather than two, and instead of slavery they now pay their colored servants ten cents a day so nobody can confuse them with slaves. I'm sure my father thinks even that's too much. That was the only real problem we ever had—the war. My brother fought for the South. My only feeling was that I just wanted to find some other solution than all the killing that went on."

Whatever melancholy had been in her voice and eyes went hard when I talked about the war. Now, voice and eyes were even tighter, harder. "David said that you were both spies and assassins."

"It was war. There were some people we had to kill to win. That's how the South felt about it and that's how we felt about it. I used to have a boss who was a Pinkerton. He always said, 'What you have to remember, son, is that this is nothin' personal. You're killin' them just because it's your job.' I used to think he was crazy, but by the end of the war I figured he was right."

I knew I'd made a mistake even before I'd finished speaking. Her eyes filled with tears and a tiny sob caught in her throat.

"I wish you hadn't told me that," she said, pulling away from me. " 'Nothing personal.' I don't like to think of either you or David that way."

I watched until she was inside and lamplight bloomed in the window. Then I headed back to town, where the two men hiding in the alley found me and tried to beat my head in without quite doing me the service of killing me.

Chapter 10

They knew what they were doing.

They had apparently followed me for some time as I walked Jane to her place. They gambled that I would take the same route home, just reversed. Therefore, it made sense for them to wait in the alley. Therefore, it made sense for them to wear dark kerchiefs over their faces and low-riding wide-brimmed hats that would shadow even their eyes. Therefore, it made sense for them to lunge at me before I'd even crossed the mouth of the alley.

I had no time to react, especially not with my arm in a sling. I heard them and started to turn backward to see what they were doing—the scraping sound on the sandy alley soil told me that they were basically running for me, so instinctively I knew I was being assaulted—but by the time I was able to get my first glimpse of them one kicked me straight in the groin and the other one grabbed me around the neck with such force that I was in perfect position for the ball-kicker to crack his Colt across my head two or three times and send me off into the realm of cold darkness.

They'd blindfolded me. They'd lashed me to a straight-backed chair. They'd dumped several gallons of water on me. I was shivering.

My wound hurt, my groin hurt, my head hurt. I wasn't so much afraid as I was mad—mad at them for obvious reasons, but also mad at myself. Maybe I couldn't have stopped them from grabbing me, but I should have been a lot more aware of my circumstances. I'd been thinking about Jane, which I shouldn't have been doing in the first place.

"Give him some more water."

Man's voice. Raspy with tobacco and whiskey.

Clank of a bucket handle. Grunt from the man lifting it.

Cold angry splash of water all over my head and most of my torso.

The splasher said: "Better be careful we don't drown him."

Bossman: "We want him good and cold. We used to do this to them stinkin' Rebs all the time. They'd get so cold they'd tell you anything you want to hear."

Splasher (walking right up to my face): "Where's the fuckin' gun, you asshole? The one your brother had." Giggling. To Bossman: "Lookit that sumbitch shake."

Bossman walking across the wooden floor, closer to me.

Where was I? Somewhere near the railroad yard. I could hear cars being switched to sidings in the long, dark, lonely, prairie night. Men shouting back and forth to each other; men at work. Probably somewhere near the big barn the railroad used for repairs.

Bossman: "Where's the gun?"

"I don't know." I had to clear my voice and repeat myself. "I don't know. How about shutting the window?"

"Sure," Splasher said. "And then how about a nice steak and then a nice big farm gal for some pussy?"

Bossman: "The window's open to keep you nice and chilly, Ford. You should see yourself. You're shakin' all over."

Splasher put his face up to mine again. "Where's the fuckin' gun, you asshole?" Good ol' Splash. He was obviously the bright one of the two.

Bossman: "Don't mind him. He's getting cold, too. Just wants to close that window and get warm, same as you and me. Go get some more water from the creek."

Splasher: "Shit, I just got some."

Bossman: "You don't want to be here all night, do you? Now hurry up."

Splasher muttered under his breath and picked up the clanking bucket and then went out, slamming the door.

Mention of the creek fixed the location for sure. Down behind the railroad barn ran a narrow creek that was deep enough for the workers to dive into when the summer heat got too much at night.

Bossman: "I was fooling you. We're cold as hell, too. We'll all end up with pneumonia, we're not careful."

"I don't know where the gun is."

"He was your brother."

"I still don't know where it is. The last time I saw it, he was demonstrating it to the four men who were interested in buying it. No doubt one of them is probably paying you to work me over like this."

It's hard to convey what my voice sounded like. My teeth were literally chattering and my voice was wavering up and down so raggedly that not all of the words came out clear.

"You like a smoke, Ford?"

"Is that a trick question? Of course I'd like a smoke."

"I'm afraid your makings are pretty soaked. But how about I give you one of mine? One of those pre-rolled smokes."

"I'll take it."

And I did. I was shaking so hard the cigarette fell out of my mouth before he got it lighted. Then I got the cigarette so soaked from hair dripping water that he had to pitch it and give me another one. And then I finally started taking sweet, pure smoke into my lungs.

"Where the hell's that water at, anyway?"

The gunshot. One of them. Loud, lone. A muffled shout.

"What the hell was that?" Bossman said.

Walked to the door. Door creaking open.

"Where the hell is he?" Bossman, turning back to me: "You don't try nothin' funny."

"What could I try?" I shivered, speaking around my cigarette.

He went outdoors. Footsteps on dry ground. Retreating. Searching.

I was curious, too, of course. Send a man out for a bucket of water to a nearby creek, how long could it take him? Then a gunshot. What was going on?

I smoked the cigarette down to the nub. The flame was about to burn my lips. I finally had to spit it out. With my arms tied tight to my torso, I didn't have a hand to use. The arm in the sling was numb by now. They'd cinched the rope around me too tight. Not that this would have broken their hearts. They'd figure the extra pain would just get me to tell them about the gun. You read in books and stories how men, and sometimes women, stand up to hours of torture. I'm always chary of such claims. They know how to break you. It's trial and error; it's duration. Either they find the precise method to break you or they keep trying different methods until you snap from sheer exhaustion. I'm sure there are men and women who've stood up to whatever torture was imposed on them. But I doubt there are many of them.

Another gunshot. No muffled scream this time. Wind seemed to hide what sounded vaguely like a heavy weight slamming against the ground.

Then just wind. Showing off a little, I guess. Rattling trees, spraying sandy soil against the cabin I was in, whipping up the prelude to a real rainstorm.—little drops of water blown against my already wet face.

No human sounds. No animal sounds. The wind hiding the noises of the railroad barn.

Becoming aware again of how cold I was. Sneezing. My throat already burning. I'd always had tonsil trouble.

Fuckers. You know how you get when you're getting sick. At least I do. Irrational rage. A reasonable amount of pain, I can handle. But not being sick. I didn't care so much now that they'd beaten me, kidnapped me, tied me up, demanded to know where the gun was. I wanted to get my hands on them and beat them to death—literally, at this point in my rage—because in addition to the gunshot wound and the sling holding me down, I would now have a bad cold that was bound to slow me down. Assuming they didn't kill me.

Somebody in the doorway. A faint shoe-scraping sound. Then no sound at all except the wind. Pictured somebody in the door frame. Watching me.

"Hello," I said.

But there was no answer. Footsteps coming across the floor. The man who'd fired the shots outside? "Hello," I said again. But this time the wind took my voice. My strength left, too.

The darkness . . . just the darkness.

Chapter 11

Delirium. Pastpresent. Images of my lifetime merging. Remorse, bliss, fear, remorse.

Traveling. Bumpy road. My guess: bed of buckboard. Awareness: wound hurting. Scratchy blankets. Voice. Voices.

Scents: lamp oil, medicine, woman.

Voices.

"I'm telling you, Marshal, he's not in his right mind. Most of the time he just babbles. You'll need to wait till morning before you talk to him. Late morning."

"His memory'd be fresher now."

Shivering again. Entire body. Pastpresent. Images of my lifetime merging.

"Now, Marshal, please do what I say and go the hell on home."

Laugh. "You make a persuasive case, Doc. You should've been a lawyer."

"Careful now or I'll wash your mouth out with soap."

Healing from the wound, I'd gotten broth and bits of bread.

From the beating and the dousing I'd taken last night, I got coffee, two thick slices of ham, three eggs and a huge slice of bread gleaming with fresh strawberry preserves.

I also got Nurse Jane.

"You could've died if the marshal hadn't found you in that cabin."

I was busy eating—I imagined I was making a lot of noise smacking my lips and I didn't give a damn—which wasn't all that easy with one good arm. Shoveling food in your mouth usually takes two hands, at least at the rate I was jamming it in.

"Somebody killed the two men who kidnapped you."

"You know who the men were?"

"Around here, everybody knows who they were. Their names were Bines and Selkirk. They were the last two of a gang that used to rob banks here in the Territory. That was what most people said, anyway. They lived here the past six or seven months and they were always in trouble for little things, mostly involving fights when they got drunk. One time they beat up this other prisoner in jail so badly he nearly died. The marshal got in the cell with them and then beat Bines bad enough to break his nose and two ribs. The marshal hated them."

I paused, started to speak.

She said, "You have a piece of egg hanging off your nose."

"I'll bet I look pretty handsome."

"Let me get it for you." She dipped a napkin into my water glass and then cleaned me up. The way a mom would.

I thanked her. "They wanted to know where David hid the gun."

"Everybody in town wants to know where David hid the gun. It's all anybody talks about. They even stop me in the street. They think maybe he told me without telling me."

"How's that again?"

"You know. They think David probably gave me a hint of where he hid it and that I'll be walking along the street someday and it'll just come to my mind. Meanwhile, they have all these guesses as to where it might be. That's what they always tell me, their guesses."

"The gun could be long gone."

"That's what I tell them."

"Or one of the four men who came to town to buy may have it and be hiding it somewhere."

"I tell them that, too. But they don't listen. I imagine the gold rush days were like that here. Everybody half-crazy thinking they'll get rich if they can just find it."

"How's Fairbain?"

"About the same. Still unconscious. But he's not getting any worse, anyway."

"I wish I knew who beat him."

"So does Marshal Wickham. He's here twice a day."

I looked at the empty dishes. "When do I get out of here?"

"The doctor said that he wants to look at you later this afternoon. Then he'll probably let you go. You have a slight concussion. That head of yours can't take much more punishment. And you've got a slight cold. You could've gotten pneumonia."

I yawned. All the good food had made me logy. But at least the cold wasn't as bad as I'd feared.

She swept up the dishes with her usual skill and said, "The marshal'll be here in an hour or so. You should take a little nap."

"I don't know if I'm that tired."

Two minutes after she left my room I was asleep.

I could hear Marshal Wickham glad-handing the hospital staff from the front door all the way to my room. The good ones run for office 365 days a year, not just at election time. Smiles and handshakes and friendly hellos are remembered a lot longer than speeches and reelection fliers, and Marshall Wickham had obviously learned that a long time ago. I'd met a lawman just outside Kansas City who personally delivered donated groceries to poor families. And when the snows came, he spent the day shoveling paths to old folks and invalids. These are the good ones. The bad ones don't usually last long enough to matter.

He must have been after my vote, too, because even before he said anything he put a sack of Bull Durham and some cigarette papers on the stand next to my bed.

"No need to thank me for saving your life," he said. And then laughed. "They were a pair, weren't they?"

"Thought I had the gun. Or the man who hired them did, anyway."

"I still haven't figured out who that was yet. One

of the arms fellas, for sure. But I figure that between us we can figure out who it is."

"Between us? You mean work together?"

"Sure. Why not? You got this notion that you Federales and local law can't work together. I'm here to show you otherwise."

"I thought you thought I tried to kill Fairbain?"

"Crossed my mind, I'll admit that. But then I started realizing that you wouldn't have any particular reason to kill him. Then when I saw you tied up in that chair . . ." He made a gift of his big hand. His palm was as coarse as old leather. "Well, I can only hold these arms fellas a few more days. Once they're gone, we'll never be able to figure anything out."

"I agree with you there."

"Doc tells me you need a good night's sleep. When you get yourself ready in the morning, stop in and see me. I may be in court. The county attorney brought charges against this land developer who took all this money from some locals and then never got around to developing any land."

"I could see where that would tend to piss somebody off."

"Yeah, just a mite, especially if it was your life savings you handed over to him." He grinned. "Now get some sleep. And when you wake up, Jane'll be here taking care of you. No wonder you like this place so much."

After he left, I turned the lamp down and lay there thinking about the gun. It didn't weigh that much, it wasn't pretty except for its ability to fire a few more bullets with a little more precision, the mechanics of it weren't even all that different from the existing Gatling model. But men, intelligent men, chased it the way they chased that beautiful woman who'd always just eluded them, the woman glimpsed on a sunny street, or in a dim train window or turned into a work of art on canvas. There was an almost sexual fervor about the chase for the gun. The difference being that the chase for the woman inspired beauty; the chase for the gun inspired death.

I had a smoke and thought about Jane for a time. Finally, the gods merciful, I slept the peaceful sleep of a ten-year-old who'd exhausted himself swimming and playing baseball all day.

What was supposed to be a routine surgery went bad in the morning—the doctor had ended up keeping me overnight—and the hospital became a grim and frenzied place. Both doctors and all three nurses spent the time in surgery trying to save the man's life. I hadn't been told what had gone wrong. I probably wouldn't have understood, anyway. I took a sponge bath, shaved, dressed in clothes some helpful citizen had brought over from my hotel room, and then left the hospital in search of the world's finest breakfast.

What were probably pretty ordinary eggs, ham, and sliced potatoes tasted like something not even a king should expect. The coffee, four cups of it, went down mighty fine, too. The last cup went down even better with a cigarette I rolled from the Bull Durham Wickham had given me. For the length of time it took me to burn the cigarette down, I thought back through the investigation so far and realized that I hadn't spent much time at all at the ranch where David had lived for so many months. I needed to go back through everything, step by step, and then catch myself up to date. I reasoned the way Wickham did. We didn't have much time left to hold the four men who'd come here to bid on the gun. We had to get going.

Turned out Wickham, as he'd suspected, had gotten tied up in court. I went over to the livery and got myself a saddle and a horse and headed out for the ranch. Real fall was setting in. Despite the blinding beauty of the golden red leaves and the clean, blue sky and the pastoral look of farmers following plow and horse as they tilled their land, the bite of winter was on the air. It was nearly eleven a.m. and the temperature was around forty, and despite the full, clear sun there was no promise of it getting any hotter.

When I reached the crest of the hill that looked down on the ranch, I wondered for the first time if David had found any peace here. We'd always been a restless pair. And though we'd grown up on a plantation packed with privilege for two little white boys, there'd always been a streak of unhappiness in us. Every once in a while, and for no particular reason, my mother would go upstairs and close the door on her sewing room and sob. There was never any explanation for it. One time I heard my father trying to soothe her: "I wish you knew why these damned moods came on you, Susan." And she'd said: "I can't even explain them to myself, dear." Maybe it was Mother's blood that explained the unhappiness, the restlessness, the sense that happiness was motion. If you could run fast enough and far enough it wouldn't catch up with you.

I made my slow and careful way up to the ranch house. I avoided the barn. I had to work up to that.

Images of David with his throat slashed—I went through the house first. I was inside for maybe a half hour—not turning up much—when I heard him.

What he did was trip over a section of drainpipe on the ground. I didn't realize this at first, of course. All I knew was that somebody was outside, at the back of the house, and that he was making some kind of noise. I slipped my gun from my holster and went to have a look.

I found him on the side of the house, his hand to his forehead like a visor, peering in through the window.

"If you're looking for me, I'm right here."

He was maybe five feet tall, with a shiny, bald head and a pair of store-boughts that clacked even when he wasn't talking. He wore a faded, red, woolen shirt and a filthy pair of butternuts. He had a knife the size of a sword stuck through the front of his belt. I could smell him from ten feet away. "Where's Ford?"

"I'm Ford."

"The hell you say. You ain't Ford."

"I'm Noah Ford."

"Noah Ford?" He made it sound as if the concept that there could be two Fords on the planet was just too much for him to deal with. "This some kind of trick?"

"No. I'm his brother. Or was. He's dead."

"He's dead? That sonofabitch."

Despite the stench, which was considerable, I moved closer to him. "I'd be careful if I was you. Like I said, he was my brother."

"Yeah? Well, mister, he owed me money. So that makes him a sonofabitch in my book."

"Who the hell are you?"

"Hobbins. Wylie Hobbins."

I stopped moving toward him. The odor halted me.

"I got this skin disease is what you're smellin'. It looks even worse than it smells. This here woman saw me without my shirt on and she fainted dead away, and that ain't no bullshit." He grinned with his store-boughts. "It's my secret weapon."

"What did he owe you money for?"

"Trips to the island. I took him three times."

"What island?"

"Parson's Cairn." He winked at me. "That's where he took the married ones."

"He was seeing married women?"

"Yep, two of them. I'd take David and one of them over on the raft and then come back for them a couple hours later. I'll tell you one thing, he sure didn't like to pay his bills. From what I hear, he run up debts all over the place."

I'd forgotten that. Because of the way we'd been raised, David had this notion that people he considered to be commoners—which was basically everybody except our family—should be just double-damned delighted to wait on us and do our bidding in any way we saw fit. And if they wanted to get paid for these services? Well, sir, it just depended on his mood. Or if he liked you. Or if your coarseness didn't in some way offend his high-born sensibilities.

So David had owed a lot of people money. No surprise.

"How much did he owe you?"

He told me. I dug in my pocket, brought out a nice, shiny, gold coin and flipped it to him. "There you go."

He caught it, looked at it this way and that, a real

trusting gent, shrugged, and put it in his pocket. "Who killed him? Some pissed-off husband?"

"I'm not sure yet."

"You can bet it was a husband, the way he caroused around. He was one of them fellas that just couldn't keep his hands off other people's property."

"Maybe I could invite you to his funeral and you could pay him a tribute." But sarcasm was too subtle for this one. "You got the names of the two women he took to the island?"

"You got another one of them gold eagles?"

I wanted to hit him but I had to figure out a way of doing it without touching him. The stench was rotting flesh. I pictured leprosy or some variation of it.

I flipped him another coin.

"Paulie, Stu Paulie's wife, Della. That was one. And Don Hester's wife, Irene. That was the other. But they won't do you no good."

"Why not?"

"Both moved away. Just picked up and left. Whole families and everything. Don Hester had him a nice hardware business, too. But the shame was too much. Irene Hester, she got mad when she found out about Della Paulie sneakin' off with your brother and she went right to Della's husband and told him what his wife was up to. He went to your brother and beat him up pretty bad. Bad enough that he got your brother to tell him about Irene Hester, too." He was flipping his second gold coin in the air. Sunlight caught it and as it tumbled in the soft, blue air it was the color of flame. "The Hesters packed up and left about a year ago. The Paulies left about three months after. Just couldn't take all the whispers, I reckon. You know how a small town is."

"You had yourself a pretty good day."

He gave the gold coin another toss and said, "I shoulda been doin' business with you 'stead of your brother. I like the way you pay up real prompt and all."

I couldn't handle him anymore. "Get the hell out of here."

The store-boughts clacked as he laughed. "Ain't my fault your brother was a no-account." He started to turn away and said, "You ever need me for anything, you just ask for Wylie Hobbins. People'll point you to where I am."

Yeah, I thought, they can tell by the smell.

I waved him away with great disgust.

"He was somethin', that brother of yours," he giggled over his shoulder, walking away. "He sure as hell was."

I returned to town without anything to show for the trip, except for losing a little money to Wylie Hobbins. The first place I went was the hospital. I wanted to see if Fairbain had come to yet or if he was still in a coma. I wanted to talk to Jane, too, but she was busy helping a very old lady walk down the first-floor corridor. My morning's bad luck held fast. Fairbain was still unconscious. I supposed it was even worse luck for him.

He was waiting for me outside. At first I didn't recognize him in the ten-gallon hat. On him it was comical. A New York cowboy, as they were known.

"Had any lunch, Mr. Ford?"

"Oh, it's you. I just went to see your friend, Wayland."

"Oh, c'mon now, if you mean Fairbain, he's no friend of mine. He's no friend of anybody's. And neither am I. Not anybody who's in my business, anyway. We're competitors and nothing more and nothing less. Now, how about some lunch?"

Two good reasons to take up his offer: I wondered what he wanted and I was hungry. "All right."

"Up for something fancy?" That was when I realized he'd had a few drinks. He was acting a little tougher than usual.

"Chili's about as fancy as I feel right now."

"Cold day, hot chili. Let's try that café over there."

A couple of merchants were putting election signs in their windows. Just in case you don't think the Wild West is dead and gone—if it ever really existed—the signs would convince you otherwise. A man named McLaren was running on three issues: a better school, better garbage collection, and better care of the streets. You can bet that the likes of Wild Bill Hickok and Jesse James never once gave a thought to any of these matters.

The chili was advertised as "Texas chili," and while it wasn't as hot as all that, it did make your esophagus plead for mercy at least a couple of times.

"You're showing me the sights, Mr. Ford."

"How would that be?"

"Place like this."

"I don't follow you."

"Look around. Salt of the earth. Working men. Sleeves rolled up. Heavy clothes so they can work outdoors in chilly weather. Grateful that they've got a job. They're the backbone of this country."

"You're an arrogant sonofabitch."

His head jerked back a bit, as if something had just

bit him. "What's that supposed to mean? Salt of the earth? Backbone of this country? What's wrong with that?"

"You make them sound stupid. Like pack mules. Do their jobs, salute the flag, give thanks to all millionaires who don't pay them enough for the work they do or the chances they take."

His smirk didn't surprise me. "I wonder if the Army knows that they have a labor agitator on the payroll."

"Don't fool yourself. A lot of people who don't have anything to do with labor think the way I do. We just saw the last part of the railroad west being built. All the men who died building it so the rich men could get richer. Especially the Chinese who died. The railroad people didn't even bother to keep count of them."

We were finished with our chili. We'd sat back, he with a pipe and I with a cigarette. His hat got a couple of amused glances from a burly bald guy on his way out the door.

"I guess I'll have to be very careful of how I approach you, won't I?"

"Approach me for what?"

"For selling me the gun."

"I don't have the gun."

"You're his brother."

"Is that supposed to mean something?"

"You were out there when he died. You were there because he had the gun and because he was your brother."

"I still don't see what you're driving at."

"Well, let's suppose you're a man who's tired of what he's doing. I don't mean to be churlish about this, but you look pretty worn out, Mr. Ford. The years are catching up with you."

I laughed at how obvious he had gotten all of a sudden. "So you're worried about me. You think I should retire and buy myself a cabin somewhere and finish out my years catching fish and knocking back some good whiskey."

"Or living in a nice big city with a lot of nice big ladies in it and plenty of other diversions like gambling and musicales and . . ."

I shook my head. "No point in going on. I don't have the gun. I don't know where the gun is. And even if I did have the gun I wouldn't give you or anybody else a bid because my plan is to take the gun back to the Army Department in Washington, which is the rightful owner."

"You surprise me, Mr. Ford."

I stood up and tossed some coins on the table. "Well, you don't surprise me, Mr. Wayland. You're just the kind of whore I thought you were. You might even have killed my brother, Mr. Wayland." I picked up my hat, cinched it on tight. "And God help you if you did."

Chapter 12

That afternoon the hospital was quiet. No nurses bustling about; no patients slowly walking the halls; no relatives quietly weeping.

In the small room that the docs and nurses used for eating and relaxing, I found Jane reading a magazine. When she became aware of me, she looked up and smiled. "You're starting to get some color back in your face."

The room, like every room in the hospital, was painted white. A skeleton stood in the corner, the attitude of its long bones suggesting that it was about to break into a dance. The walls were covered with lithographs of great figures in medicine. Most of them I hadn't heard of. Which made us even up, I suppose. They probably hadn't heard of me, either.

"Help yourself to the coffee," she said, before I had a chance to speak.

I poured myself a cup. In a room somewhere on the first floor, a patient coughed. It was the loudest noise I'd heard since coming here.

"Quiet," I said.

She smiled. "You're witnessing a miracle. Most of

the patients are sleeping. Dr. Roussel even had time to look for a birthday present for his little daughter. He said to mark this day on our calendars."

I angled my chair so that I could stretch my legs out. "I was out at David's place earlier today."

It's funny the effect a single word can have on the right person. Just the mention of his name changed her entire being. The head raised up a bit higher; apprehension—maybe even dread—showed in the lovely eyes; and the lips parted dryly. I imagined her pulse rate went up, too.

"You know some man named Hobbins?"

She put her magazine down. "Hobbins? No, I don't think so."

"Claims he took David to a place called Parson's Cairn. You know where that is?"

"It's on this tiny island downstream. In the early days some river pirates hid there. The story is that they buried treasure somewhere on the cairn."

"Local legend?"

"I think so. Nobody's ever found anything there that I know of."

"So David never mentioned Hobbins or Parson's Cairn?"

"Not that I remember."

I sipped coffee.

She said, "There's something you want to tell me. Or ask me."

"What makes you think that?"

"You seem nervous. That's not like you. And then you just show up and ask me questions about somebody named Hobbins and Parson's Cairn."

One of the other nurses came in. She nodded to both of us and then went to a cupboard where she found some hard candy. "Mr. Daly will be waking up soon. This'll be the first thing he asks for." The voice was fond. "He's like a little kid about his candy."

She left.

"So what is it?"

"What is what?"

"Oh, c'mon, Noah, say what you came here to say."

I sighed. Raised my eyes to look at the colorful leaves just outside the window. Merry as children, they looked.

"This Hobbins—and he may have been lying—he told me that David used to take married women to the island."

The hospital got even quieter. She began to fidget with her fingers. She stared at them as if they were creatures somehow separate from her and she was curious about what they'd do next. "Do I really need to hear the rest?"

"I'm trying to find out who killed him, Jane."

"One of those men who wanted the gun."

"Maybe. Probably. But I have to make sure." I leaned forward. I brushed her hand with mine. "I'm sorry I have to ask you this."

She didn't raise her head. "I'm sorry you have to ask me, too."

"So you think it's true?"

She nodded.

"You heard the talk? Hobbins told me that there were two women. When everybody in town figured out that they were seeing David, their husbands packed up the families and they moved."

The pretty face came into view again. "There was a man there one day just when I was riding in. He was shouting at David. And waving a pistol at him. Threatening him. I never was sure what he was so mad about. Not then, I wasn't. But then Della Paulie and her husband—they had a very public argument one day. Right after church, in fact. A lot of people heard it. And one day as I was leaving David's place, I saw a woman on a horse sort of hiding on the edge of the woods—it was the Paulie woman. So I pretty much knew then that David was the man involved."

"Did you tell him you knew?"

"No—not right away. But I must have been acting withdrawn or something, because one night he made me talk about it. He said he was tired of the way I was acting. That he expected to have fun with me, but that I'd become this really cold person. So I told him."

I knew what she would say then because I'd grown up with David and knew how he reacted any time he was accused of something that he was guilty of.

"I guess I was pretty naïve. I thought he'd tell me that he was sorry or something like that. But instead he got really mad. Told me to go home. Told me that it wasn't any of my business. Told me that I didn't have any right to question what he did."

Pure David. Change the subject. Put you on trial instead of him. Twist things to the point where you almost wanted to apologize to him for bringing it up in the first place.

The scream.

The scream that ended the quiet. The scream that set feet to running, not only on the first floor, but down the steps from the second floor. The scream that ignited a dozen startled conversations.

Jane was up out of her chair so quickly that she knocked the chair over behind her. She didn't so much as glance at me, let alone say anything. She simply took off running.

Whoever had screamed was now shouting "Dr. Hopkins! Dr. Hopkins!"

Jane wasn't in the hall. I stood outside the break room watching half a dozen people hurry through an open door near the front of the hospital.

A male voice, stern and angry: "How the hell did this happen?"

A low buzz of voices. From what I could hear, none of the other people in the room had anything meaningful to say. They just babbled words that hoped to quell the anger of the male voice.

I eased myself down to the room where everything was going on. A cleaning woman charged out of there, knocking against me, not saying a word. Her face was frozen in shock.

I'd been so caught up in the melee that the room number hadn't registered. This was Fairbain's room. I stood behind three hospital workers who were leaning in for a look. The doc blocked my view of Fairbain's head and upper torso. But from the chest down it was easy to see that Fairbain was having convulsions. His body jumped and jerked with so much force that the bed itself was moving at an angle. The doc shouted to Jane and another nurse, "Hold this bed down!"

I pushed past the workers and crowded my way inside. I grabbed the metal end of the bed and held on to it. Jane and the other nurse were anchoring the head of the bed. The doc glanced up at me and glowered, but went right back to his work.

Fairbain's face was a greenish color. His blue eyes stared hard at the ceiling. There was madness in them. He had puked all over himself. Vomit was still dribbling out of the right side of his mouth. The vomit was a deeper green than the color of his face. His face was glazed with sweat. His teeth clacked, his body was shaking so hard. The part of me that stays detached at moments like these—I suppose it's a way of not fully registering the horror I'm witnessing—wondered what kind of poison somebody had given him. Not that it mattered. There would be a medical examination and the poison would be given a name and that name would be read to the judge, but the name didn't matter to anybody but the docs and the lawyers. What mattered, to me anyway, is that the one man who might have been able to identify the killer was just a few seconds from dying. The one man who'd offered some small hope now offered no hope at all.

His convulsing stopped. One moment he was death-dancing all over his bed and then he was corpse-still. But his labored breathing—coming in snorts now, snorts that expelled long strings of wet snot from both his nostrils—his breathing had a rattle to it now and there was no doubt about what that meant.

The doc stopped, too. "Somebody's going to lose their job over this," he said, glaring at Jane and the other nurse. Then he glared at me. "And just who the hell are you?" He needed to unload his rage, his failure, and I probably looked like the deserving type.

I showed him my badge.

"You think I can read that sonofabitch from here? What kind of badge is it?"

Fairbain's bowels exploded then. The smell made everybody move back a foot or two from the bed. The body convulsed again a few times as well.

"It says I'm an Army investigator."

"Oh," he said, "so you're Ford."

"That's right."

He was finding his emotional footing again. He took a deep breath. Let it out. "Marshal Wickham mentioned you. Sorry I didn't recognize you."

He nodded to Jane and the other nurse. "Sorry I was yelling, ladies. Someday somebody's going to take me seriously about security in this place. I keep telling the Board that this place is wide open to anybody who wants to come in here. And now we see what can happen."

He was still angry, but now he was angry at a lower and more socially acceptable decibel. The nurses offered him sympathetic gazes and I nodded my head and said, "You have to have security everywhere these days." Now there was a brainstorm, but the doc was so het up I thought I'd agree with him on general principle.

He glanced down at Fairbain. "Tell Rooney to run and get the marshal, would you, Marge?"

"Of course, Doctor."

Two male workers came in with buckets and mops and bleach, followed by a nursing assistant with fresh bedclothes. The various smells were starting to accumulate.

To the nursing assistant, the doc said, "Open the window and then close the door. Let this air out for at least eight hours."

"Yes, Doctor."

He glanced at me. "I need to consult with the other doctor, Mr. Ford. He knows a lot more about poisons than I do."

Jane found me on the back porch. She went over to the edge of it and looked down at a buckboard filled with boxes that were being offloaded by two Mexican men. Her eyes were slick with tears.

We stood in a far corner. I rolled a cigarette. She'd taken to staring down at her fidgeting fingers again. I knew better than to say anything. She'd speak in her own time.

"I've never seen anybody die that way."

"Me, either," I said.

"You think you're pretty much used to everything—you know, after being a nurse for six years and everything—but then something like this happens." She touched my arm. "It's about the gun, isn't it?"

"I guess so. It would seem to be. That's why Fairbain came to town. He wasn't here long enough the first time or this time to really get to know anybody. So I suppose somebody poisoned him for the gun. But it doesn't make sense when you think about it."

"Maybe Fairbain knew something and the killer didn't want him to talk to you."

"That's about the only thing I can figure, too."

"Maybe he knew where the gun was. Maybe he had a partner. Maybe the partner killed him because he didn't want a partner anymore."

Then she leaned into me—the only parts of our bodies really touching were our arms—but there was a gentle intimacy in the move, and we stood there

silent for a time, letting our bodies speak much more
eloquently than our tongues ever could.

A nurse came then and said quietly, "Jane. We
need you."

Jane left immediately.

Chapter 13

I met Marshal Wickham on the steps outside.

"You figured anything out yet?" he asked.

"He was poisoned."

"No wonder they pay you Federales so much money. Bright ideas like that."

"I guess that's about all anybody knows about it at the moment."

He raised his head, his eyes taking in the front of the hospital. "You could sneak an army into that place."

"Yeah, they were talking about that."

He scowled. "Fairbain must've known something."

"Might have."

Deputy Frank Clarion came walking toward us, fast. The next minute or so showed me how well the two men worked together. They didn't say much, didn't need to. That comes from years of working together, competent years.

"I heard about Fairbain," Clarion said.

"Yeah."

"You talked to the people inside yet?"

"You're better at that sort of thing."

All Clarion did was nod and then glance at me, as if seeing me for the first time. "How's the shoulder?"

"A little better every day."

"Good."

He walked upstairs, went indoors.

"He's a good man," Wickham said. Then he grinned. "Even if he is my nephew."

It didn't take long to find Wayland, Brinkley, and Spenser. They sat around a large table in the back of the restaurant in the hotel. They weren't talking, which meant that they'd heard about Fairbain.

"You aren't welcome to sit down," Spenser said.

"Oh, for God's sake," Wayland said, "sit down, Ford."

Brinkley shrugged.

I considered ordering food, but then I remembered the color and texture of Fairbain's vomit and I wasn't hungry at all.

His death apparently didn't have much effect on the other men's appetites. They ordered the special, which was mutton, along with a loaf of hot bread and boiled potatoes with gravy.

I said, "One of you could clear this whole thing up pretty fast."

"And how would that be?" Brinkley said. A stray beam of sunlight caught the birthmark on his cheek, turning it a vicious red.

"Well, one of you killed Fairbain. Maybe two of you. Whichever one of you three is innocent is probably going to die next."

"I want to digest my food," Spenser said, an enormous man of enormous anger. "Which will be impossible if I have to listen to this nonsense."

"Then who killed Fairbain?" I said.

"How the hell would I know who killed Fairbain?" Spenser said.

"Somebody who wanted the gun," I said.

"Have you ever considered," said Brinkley, looking more like a sour minister than ever, "that there could be someone else in town who knows about the gun—someone who wants it as bad as we do—someone Fairbain saw and could identify."

"A possibility, I suppose. But you three are still at the top of the list."

"Why did you ask this damned fool to sit down?" Spenser snapped at Wayland. "Are you happy now?"

"I thought it would be a little more cordial than this, I guess," Wayland said quietly. He was the least demonstrative of the three.

"Cordial," Spenser scoffed. To Brinkley he said, "Our friend Wayland doesn't seem to understand that Ford here is accusing at least one of us of murder."

I addressed my words to Wayland: "You could be the next one who gets killed, Wayland. You still want the gun and you have to play out your hand. But you're scared now. One of your friends here killed Fairbain and you know it."

Spenser laughed. "Well, at least you're playing to the right one, Ford. Wayland here is a pantywaist. You should've heard him complaining all the time on the train. Too hot, too cold, too noisy, too dangerous. I don't know how he ever got a job like this."

Wayland surprised us all by making himself even more vulnerable. He stood up, threw down his cloth napkin, and said, "Because my father is a bully just like you, Spenser, and for some reason I'll never understand I want to prove to him that I can be as successful at arms trafficking as he was."

We sat in embarrassed silence until he left.

Spenser smiled around a mouthful of lamb, not a pleasant sight. He spoke mockingly: "There's your killer, Ford. A sensitive nancy boy who just wants the love and respect of his father."

"Oh, shut the hell up, Spenser," Brinkely said. He didn't seem the kind to take the part of a weak one like Wayland, but I liked him better for doing it.

Then it was my turn to stand up. "Maybe you two'll do the world a favor and kill each other off."

Spenser said, "Does this mean you don't like us, Mr. Ford?"

You'd never have guessed that James Andrews was Cree, not by looking at his house you wouldn't. It was a two-story white clapboard arrangement with a picket fence, flowers planted across the front of the house and a swing on the porch. In back and to the side were a small red barn, an outhouse, and a rope corral. There was a long windbreak of pines on the south side of the property and a clean, narrow creek running parallel to the north.

It was some house for a man like James. It would be some house even for an attorney of middling success. I saw why his wife Gwen was suspicious of where the money had come from. She'd left a note at my hotel for me to come see her.

Except for a breeze gently swaying the pines, the

place was silent. Even the lone bay in the rope corral was napping.

I dismounted, grabbing my carbine from the scabbard as I did so. There had been a number of deaths in a short span of time in this town. The general feeling seemed to be that there would be more.

The family watchdog proved to be a sweet-faced border collie. I presented her with a tough decision. She knew she should bark, so she did, at least a bit. But she seemed more inclined to jump at me and lick my hand. She seemed starved for human company. She opted for the latter, running in circles around me till I relented, bent over, and started petting her.

She trotted alongside me as I went through the gate in the picket fence and made my way to the front door. Nobody answered my knock. I walked over to the window, my boots and spurs making way too much noise for the stealthy investigator. I peeked inside. Nicely furnished front room and behind that a small dining room. I expected the kitchen would be beyond, in the back. A yellow cat came strolling out of nowhere, walked to the center of the front room, extended its paws, had a nice stretch, a nice yawn, and then lay down and went immediately to sleep. If it had seen me, it hadn't been much impressed.

A clattering sound came from the south, beyond the windbreak. A rickety old wagon of some kind, I suspected.

Gwen Andrews waved at me as soon as she reached the edge of her property. I'd walked around to the side of the house to wait for her. She had a young girl next to her on the seat of the buckboard. Everything on the wagon made a noise. You got the impression that someday the thing would just fall apart.

She pulled up, jumped down, grabbed the small girl in the gingham dress and matching bonnet. She set the girl down on her feet and then took her hand and brought her over to me.

"This is Julia."

"Hi, Julia."

She was a rough draft of her mother, Julia was. The same piquancy in the eyes and on the mouth. The same sinewy body, same tanned face and arms. A farm girl with an appealing, freckled, prairie face.

Julia didn't say hi, just shyly stood next to her mother with her head down. She looked to be about five.

"I was going to come to town to see you," Gwen said.

"Something come up?"

"Maybe. Why don't you come inside? The little one here needs her nap and I need my coffee. How's that sound?"

It sounded fine. Julia was asleep in Gwen's arms even before we reached the back door of the house. A cider mill stood on the back porch, adding the scent of apples to other fall scents. Red, flawless apples filled the bin on top. On the handle, a brown cotton work glove drooped. No matter how efficient a given mill was, it could still give you blisters after a while. Next to the back door was a line of six clear glass bottles filled with the product of the mill.

Gwen put Julia to bed and came out to where I waited in the front room. I'd been studying a print of a fierce and noble Indian warrior. His eyes were terrifying, or meant to be anyway. He was supposed to be a mythic warrior, I suppose. But Indians aren't any different from white folks. Dying is too strange and spooky to allow for myth. The bravest man of all will still cry out for his mother when he's dying. That's just the way the human beast is constructed.

"There's cider, too."

"Coffee, I guess."

"Want to sit on the back porch? I'll still be able to hear Julia if she cries. It's such a nice day."

We enjoyed the breeze and the cider smell. She sat watching a hawk sail on a wind current. She wore a work shirt and dungarees, her gray-streaked black hair pulled into a loose bun. She had quite the profile and almost perfectly uptilted breasts for a woman her age. I enjoyed looking at the profile and the breasts even more than I enjoyed the scents of wind and apples.

She excused herself a moment. She returned quickly, a group of white, business-sized envelopes in her hand. She sat down and handed them over to me.

I opened the flaps on each of the four. Empty inside. Then I saw, reading the return addresses, why she wanted me to see them.

"Fairbain," she said, "New Orleans."

"He lived there when he wasn't traveling. Wife and son."

"I think there were bank drafts inside."

"What makes you think that?"

"One day when James was leaving, I saw him fold something and stick it in his pocket. I've been thinking about it since he was killed. I'm pretty sure it was a bank draft. A certified check, maybe."

"I wonder why Fairbain would send him money. If he did, I mean."

"No idea. But as I told you the other day, he did come into money all of a sudden."

"Maybe Fairbain wanted him to steal the gun," I said.

"That's what I was thinking."

"Paid him in advance. Where'd you find these envelopes?"

"Pocket of his Sunday suit. The jacket. Folded over. I think he hid them there. You know, from me."

"You said he kept secrets."

Sad, slow smile. "I'll never know the half of them."

"Odd way to pay in advance, though. Four payments. Why not all at once?"

"Maybe Fairbain couldn't raise the money all at once."

"I know the people he worked for. They have plenty of money. For a chance at the gun they would have given him just about anything he asked for."

"You can keep the envelopes."

"Thanks." Then: "You be OK?"

"Sometime in the not too distant future I will. It's Julia I'm worried about. She's had terrible nightmares the past few nights. I'm sure it's because of James dying."

I stared down at the envelopes. What did they mean? While the gun was still the focus of the investigation, the envelopes confused the issue. And I wondered about Wylie Hobbins, the odd, diseased man I'd met at David's place. Hobbins said he'd taken David to a small island many times. That seemed overcareful on David's part. Did he need to go to an island to sneak off with married women? Was the island used for something else as well?

"This has been a tough year for me," Gwen said softly. "My best friend Louise died last year. One of the sweetest people who ever walked the earth. Pretty, too. Very pretty. Slipped off a cliff and drowned."

"Did she live around here?"

Gwen pointed to the west. "Had a small cabin over on an island. At first Louise really liked it there. Then her husband and son died a few years ago. Influenza came through here just like an invading army. Killed a whole lot of people. She had some insurance money to live on, though it would've run out sooner than later." Her dark eyes glistened. "Anyway, I sure wish she was around to talk to." Then she made a self-deprecating gesture. Waved herself off. "But you didn't come here for that."

Just then Julia cried out, sounding afraid. Maybe she was having nightmares in the daytime. "I'd better check on her." She was off her chair in less than a second, headed toward the back door.

"I need to get back, too. Thanks for these envelopes."

Julia yelped again. Gwen vanished inside.

Chapter 14

Twenty minutes later I was half a mile from town. That was when my horse was shot out from under me. The shooter, hidden in some shallow woods to the south, had obviously meant to hit me but had missed.

This piece of road had buffalo grass on either side. No trees, no boulders, nowhere to hide. I had to lie flat on my belly, using the horse to hide as much of my six feet two as I could.

The first thing I did, once my heart and brain adjusted to what had happened, was shoot the animal in the top of the head. It had taken the shooter's rifle bullet in its heart and was in misery. The second thing I did was yank my carbine from its scabbard on the poor dead animal. I now had some parity with the shooter.

Flies, loose bowels, and ghoulish twitches made the horse less than the ideal hiding place. The shooter got off two more shots.

He was firing from behind some hardwoods. There was enough forest shadow to obscure him completely. A couple times I caught a sun-flash of his rifle barrel, which helped me direct my own bullets.

He apparently didn't like the idea that I was firing back, because after a quiet two or three minutes, I could hear his horse thrashing through a narrow path in the woods. And then, momentarily, the heavy thud of his horse in a clearing, pounding ground in escape.

When I was pretty sure it was safe, I stood up and began the hard and sweaty process of getting the saddle off. Try it some time, moving around the dead weight of an animal this size while trying to undo various straps and ties. I didn't like to think of what scavengers would do to its body once I started walking to town. You'd think after everything I'd seen in the war that I'd have made my peace with the innocent horror of nature, of scavengers. But it's difficult sometimes. You begin to resent animals for being animals, but it's just their nature, and that's a fool's waste of time.

It wasn't that long a walk, or wouldn't have been, without the saddle slung over my shoulder. I was just at the town limits when a farmer in a buckboard headed in my direction stopped and offered me a ride. I laughed and said that I might as well walk the rest of the way since the livery was about half a block away.

Livery stables are the second most populated places for male gossip. Barbershops are first. Saloons are third, only because most of what is said is forgotten in hangover by morning.

I was almost at the livery when I saw Beth Cave, the mortuary secretary who'd tried to tell me something about a woman named—and then I made the connection. Louise. She'd been telling me something about a woman named Louise. Just as Gwen had been talking about a woman named Louise.

Given one arm in a sling, a saddle slung over my shoulders, and pretty damned weary legs, I hurried as fast as I could to the corner she stood on.

She made a little joke, which, given her prim, taut face, surprised me. "Isn't a horse supposed to go with that saddle?"

But her joshing faded when I told her that my horse had been shot out from under me.

"Oh, I'm sorry. I shouldn't have made light of it."

I said, "You were telling me about a woman named Louise."

Her cheeks turned scarlet. "I—I shouldn't have said anything. Mr. Newcomb almost fired me."

"I'd appreciate it if you'd finish what you were going to say."

Instead of a black dress, today she wore a black suit. She was so thin, she resembled a scarecrow. "I need my job, Mr. Ford. I'm the only support of my sick father. If I ever got fired. . . ."

Tears in her eyes, her voice. "I'm sorry, Mr. Ford. Very sorry."

She hurried away, her gait awkward and somehow lonely.

By the time I set my saddle down in the barn, there must've been a dozen men standing in the sun-blasted entrance, listening to me tell my story to the livery man.

You could sense the men were disappointed. Couldn't I at least have been attacked by Indians or a bear or found myself trapped in a pit full of rattlers? Even with the horse dead, it wasn't all that much of a tale.

Then they remembered what it was possibly all about and got interested for the first time.

"That gun."

"Durn right. That's what the shooter was after."

"Probably figured Ford here was goin' after it himself."

"Wound him and make Ford take him to the gun."

"Get the gun, kill Ford, and have the gun all to himself."

"Live like a king the rest of his life."

"Frisco and gals with tits out to here."

Bret Harte had nothing on these men. In fact, if Harte ever wanted a collaborator, I knew just which livery stable to send him to.

To the livery man, as I was paying him for the horse, I said, "You could always send a wagon out there and pick him up."

The man nodded. He wore a greasy old derby on top of a greasy old head. "Yeah. Don't want his bones picked clean. Me'n the colored fella works with me'll go get him now."

"Thanks."

After stopping by my hotel for gloves and a heavier jacket, I walked over to the river and a boatyard. It was a jumble of a place, filled with rowboats, schooners, rafts, and skiffs, some of which were being repaired, some of which were up for sale. That was up front. In back was a mountain of pieces of boats, schooners, rafts, and skiffs. I doubted the owner knew what all was in that towering pile.

A big man with a long, gray beard came hobbling

out of the little shack that said SEECRAFT over the door. I hoped he was better at boating than he was at spelling.

In case you questioned his seaworthiness, he wore an eye patch, which might or might not have been for effect; and jerked about on a peg leg, which was very much for real. He might have lost his leg on a ranch or a city street, but who was I to question him? Better for both our sakes to think that he'd lost it on a pirate ship while raiding a Spanish galleon. I was like the men back at the livery. I liked a good story, too.

"He'p you?" he asked. He wore a black wool turtleneck and regulation Navy dungarees. On his right leg, the pegged one, the dungarees had been cut off right above the knee. He hadn't shaved or bathed for a while.

"You rent boats?"

"Depends."

"On what?"

"Who wants to rent it."

"For the hell of it, let's just pretend it's me."

"Watch that mouth, mister, or I'll throw your ass out of here. This is private property."

A mangy old dog dragged himself out from beneath the mountain of parts, looked around as if to see if anybody was watching, and then took a crap. We were only ten yards away. Apparently he hadn't seen us. Maybe he should have worn an eye patch, too.

"Look," I said in my best civil voice, "I need a rowboat."

"You got one arm."

"You got one leg."

"You need two arms to row."

"I'll be fine. Now do I get a boat or what?"

"For what?"

"I want to go to Parson's Cairn."

"For what?"

"For none of your fucking business, for what."

He grinned. His teeth were so rotted they were more wormy brown than white. "I just like t'test people. See how much shit they'll take."

"Yeah, well, you picked the wrong one to test."

"The cap'n, he'd always tell me to do that with the ones what wanted to sign on. Be as cranky as I could just to see if they could stand up to the way of the cap'n. He didn't want no pussies goin' to sea with us."

"Good for him. Now, how about that rowboat? You got one or not?"

"I want twenty dollars."

"Twenty dollars? That's crazy."

"How do I know you'll bring it back?"

I waved him off, sick of him, and started to turn.

"Then when you bring it back, you get fifteen of it back."

"You got one that doesn't have any holes in the bottom?"

He grinned again. "I imagine I could find one somethin' like that. Now let's see your money."

Some kids dream of running away to the circus; some dream of running away to Arabia, the land of scimitars and harem girls; and some dream of running away to sea. Personally, I never dreamed of running away to anyplace except Cindy Dunning's gazebo, where I'd hoped to hide so I could see her undress every night.

The circus was too seedy for me, Arabia was too far away, and being on water for any length of time always had the same effect on me: I got queasy. I'd take watching Cindy Dunning undress any day.

Eyepatch was right about needing two arms to row. He sent his daughter with me. Daughter might evoke pictures of a scruffy young woman who, beneath the grit and grime, was a shy and appealing piece of womanhood.

I never did find out her name. She rowed. Her biceps were bigger than mine. She had a fist-broken nose, teeth like her old man's, a baseball-sized plug of chewing tobacco laid against her right cheek, and a disposition that made Quantril's seem saintly. She was probably forty, but looked sixty. Maybe it was the gray hair that had been chopped off short and the huge forearm tattoos that were various forms of the word FRED. I decided that it probably wouldn't be a wise idea to bring up the subject of Fred, as it was obvious that she'd tried to scrub and scratch the tattoos off.

She said, "I ain't goin' on the island because the Eye-talian woman told me it was haunted."

"Fine."

"I s'pose you don't believe that."

"That the Eye-talian woman told you that or that it's haunted?"

"My pop, he told me you was a wiseacre."

"No, I don't believe it's haunted."

"Well, then I'm gonna let you find out for yourself."

"Fine."

"Don't say I never warned you."

"I won't."

"And if I hear you a-screamin', I'm rowin' right back to my daddy's boatyard."

"I wouldn't expect anything else."

"And quit lookin' at my tattoos."

"All right."

"Fred ain't none of your business."

"Fine."

"It was what my aunt called an 'unhappy episode.' She reads books is why she talks like that."

I started the process of making a cigarette one-handed. She rowed. I didn't think about haunted islands; I didn't look at her Fred tattoos; and I didn't think about her aunt who knew how to read.

It wasn't far from the boatyard, the island, and it was bigger than I'd expected. You could set up a hamlet here; maybe even a tiny town. There was enough length and width for it. It was pretty, too, with a wide, sandy beach and a stretch of autumn colors on the trees that lined the shore.

She rowed us up to the shore. Wanting to impress her with my manliness, I climbed out of the boat and dragged it up onto the sand. Pretty good for a one-hander. She didn't seem to notice.

"Don't take all day."

"I paid your daddy five dollars."

"My daddy don't have to sit here and be bored."

I spent fifteen minutes walking around the entire beach. When I got back to the boat, she said, "You ready to go back?"

"I just wanted to see what the beach was like."

"What the hell you think it's like? It's sandy."

"I'll be back."

She spat tobacco juice into the water. I'd been

wondering what she did with all that tobacco runoff in her mouth. Maybe she swallowed most of it.

I found a trail that eventually wound its way into the heart of the island and a wide clearing that ran maybe a quarter mile. In the center of the clearing was the cairn. It stood maybe ten feet tall and three feet wide. It was a craggy assemblage of pieces of stone dragged from several points near various parts of the shore. The markings on it looked Indian but not exactly Cree. Maybe Ute or Blackfeet.

A dozen yards away was a small log cabin. This was the second generation of log cabins, not just the board roof covered with sod and the shanty look of it. This had a shake shingle roof and squared timbers.

I pushed the door open and went inside. It smelled damp, apparently from recent rains. But I didn't see anything wet. The furnishings were simple but store-bought, two cots for sleeping and a couch big enough to double as another bed. The floor was finished with wood so you could sleep on that, too, if you wanted. There was a fireplace, two cupboards sparsely stocked with canned goods, a cast-iron stove for cooking, and a large steamer trunk.

There were four windows, meaning that somebody had gone to some considerable expense. Sunlight angled through the windows facing the west and in the sun splash on the floor I saw the stains.

They were the color of grapes, the stains, as if they'd been a dark red at one time, scrubbed down as much as possible and then lacquered over. I assumed they were blood stains, but since this cabin was used by men who hunted and fished, it wasn't necessarily human blood.

I was gone an hour in all. I didn't find anything

there that made me feel that the trip had been worthwhile. I'd hoped to find some connection to the gun. I wondered if any of the men who'd wanted to buy it knew about this place. They could hide it here until they were ready to leave. But I didn't find any secret hiding places in the cabin and I'd even gone back to the cairn to see if it was wide enough at its base to conceal a weapon. No luck.

When I got back to the rowboat, she was sitting on the shore Indian-legged, a .45 in her lap.

"You took your time."

"I had a lot to do. What's the gun for?"

"I got the feeling somebody was watching me."

I turned and looked at the autumn-tinted span of trees. "Somebody in there?"

"Somebody . . . or something."

"Ghosts?"

"You go ahead and laugh. You're a city boy. You don't know how spooks operate. Some Indians run away from the Trail of Tears and hid out here so the soldier boys wouldn't find them. But they found them, all right, and killed every one of them: man, woman, and child. Except for one old man, so the story goes. He built the cairn and then cut his wrists and bled on it. That way the cairn was cursed. It's his blood that haunts this place."

The Trail of Tears. The Cheyenne loved their lives in Georgia, which they considered to be a gift directly from God. The Cheyenne had long ago adopted many of the ways of the white man. They built roads, schools, churches, and had a form of democratic government. But more and more whites pushed into Georgia as part of the migration west. And they took more and more land belonging to the Cheyenne.

When gold was discovered, the Cheyenne feared they would be pushed out of their land altogether. And they were. In 1830, President Andrew Jackson, a greedy and ruthless man, helped Congress pass the Indian Removal Act. A pretty fair share of white people battled against the act, but finally had to give up. A few years later, the Cheyenne were forced to migrate west without enough food, medicine, or even horses, to make the trip safely. Many of them died. Some of them ran away, not following the others to Oklahoma where Jackson and Congress had promised abundant and fertile land. It wasn't surprising that some of them had found their way to this area and to this island. It wasn't surprising, either, that they would want to build a cairn that was a curse to the white man.

"Let's head back."

"Maybe we got the curse now. Maybe tonight somebody'll chop off our heads with an axe. They say that's what happens when his ghost pays you a visit. I wouldn't've come out here except for my daddy made me."

"You'll be fine."

She rowed us back. This time I didn't feel so emasculated about sitting with one arm in a sling while a burly lady rowed me to the far shore. I was too lost in my thinking to worry about it.

About halfway to the mainland she said, "You want to hear about Fred? It'll pass the time."

"Sure," I said. I have the ability to look right at a person and appear to be listening intently to everything they're saying. But behind my eyes and ears, I'm lost in my own world. She told me about Fred. All I can remember was that they both got an awful lot of tattoos bearing each other's name. Well, I remember a few other things, too: that he beat her, stole from her, publicly humiliated her, and made her serve a three-month jail sentence that rightly belonged to him.

"So," she said, concluding in such a way that I thought she was going to cry, "you can see why I'd love a man like that. He sure was good-lookin'."

Marshal Wickham was having a piece of apple pie and a cup of coffee when I found him in the café. His Stetson took up about half the space of the small table where he sat. He had to set it on a chair so I'd have room for my own pie and coffee.

I said, "Unless Wayland's a damned good actor, we can eliminate him."

"Why's that?"

"He tried to bribe me. Said he wanted to give me a preemptive bid for the gun."

"He thinks you've got it?"

"Apparently."

Wickham's eyes gleamed with a kind of mean humor. "You could make yourself a nice pile of money."

"I'd rather have the man who killed my brother and the gun."

"You Federal boys are what they call single-minded."

I shrugged. "Not always. Investigators get bribed off from time to time. But never when family members are involved."

"So if we eliminate Wayland . . ."

"That leaves us Spenser and Brinkley."

"I don't take much to Spenser."

"I doubt even his mother did. He's a grade-A ass-hole." I sipped the coffee. It had a nutty flavor I liked. Kind of walnut. "I've been looking into some other things."

"What other things?"

"A couple of people tell me that David wasn't killed for the gun."

"People like to talk. Passes the time. Makes them feel important. I get that all the time. Want to butter up the marshal by tellin' him something he don't know. So they come up with these stories."

"I don't doubt that. But James's wife got me to thinking about a few other ways to look at the shootout that night."

I reminded him about the money James had suddenly come into. The new house, especially.

"You know," Wickham said, sitting back and lighting up his pipe with a stick match, "I wondered about that. Where James came into that kind of money. I should have pressed him harder about that. The place isn't a palace, but it's a nice, solid house. And it'd be expensive for everybody except rich folks. But James came up with the money."

I told him about the envelopes from Fairbain.

"I'll be damned," Wickham said.

"What?"

"That's a story that might lead somewhere. You might be on to something here, Ford."

"But if David wasn't killed for the gun, who took the gun and where is it now?"

"Yeah, that's the hard angle to figure. If he wasn't killed for the gun, why would the killer take the gun?"

"Only one reason I can figure, Marshal."

"What would that be?"

"To confuse us. Make us think it was for the gun."

He smiled. It made him look ten years younger. "So that's why you Federal boys make so much money. 'Cause you can figure things out us poor old local folks couldn't get to in a month of Sundays." Then: "You got any idea why he was killed, then? If it wasn't for the gun, I mean?"

"Not yet. Maybe never. I mean, we can't rule out the possibility that it was for the gun. Sometimes the obvious reason is the right reason."

"Those envelopes sure sound interesting. Think I'll go ask Spenser about them. I don't think he hates me quite as much as he hates you."

"You trying to hurt my feelings, Marshal?"

He laughed. "Just like you said, he's a grade-A asshole. Soon as I bring up those envelopes, I'll be right at the top of his shit list, too. You can bet on that."

"Good luck."

He pulled his hat on, cinched up his gunbelt. "Maybe I'll get lucky and he'll give me a reason to shoot him."

"I'd sure hate to think about that, Marshal. A fine man like Spenser. Shoot him a couple times for me, all right?"

Chapter 15

The desk clerk said, "A Mr. Spenser was asking for you."

"Oh? When was this?"

"Maybe an hour or so ago."

"He say when he'd be back?"

"No. He just said you'd know where to find him."

This clerk was a new one for me. He was round and had a nose so red the railroads could use it at night. The eyes were nervous. They were almost as red as the nose. He'd either had a big night or some long years of big nights.

"Is everything all right?" he said.

"I think you started to say something, then stopped."

"I was just going to say something that wasn't any of my business to say." He touched pudgy fingers to his golden cravat.

"I see."

"I mean I'd say it if you said it was all right to say it."

"I've got plenty of time. Why don't you go right ahead then?"

"Well, the management here, they think I talk too

much sometimes. Say things to the guests I shouldn't." He must have sensed my impatience. "He looked scared."

"Scared."

"Yessir. The way he kept looking around, real nervous like. And when I said you weren't in—well, I know this sounds funny, but I honestly thought I saw tears in his eyes. And you should have seen his hands." He put one of his own pudgy ones out to demonstrate. He made it twitch. "Just like that."

"Thank you for telling me that."

"You're most welcome, sir. That's what I keep trying to tell the management here. That guests like to know things that you know but that they don't. Things that might be more important than they seem."

He had a strange way of talking and it was wearing me down.

I went upstairs to my room. Every once in a while the sling started to irritate me. I took it off and lay down. Hotels are generally quiet in midafternoon. Even the wagon traffic on the main street had slowed.

I was more tired than I wanted to admit to myself. You hear saloon stories of men who get shot and are up to full steam after a good night's sleep. Maybe there's a species of very special men who can do that. I belong to the plain, old, human race and there's one truth that race holds to. The older you get, the harder it is to spring back after any kind of serious injury or wound. I could take my sling off all I wanted, trying to convince myself that I was healing up real quick, but sleep came so fast and so hard that there was no denying my exhaustion. And it wasn't yet three p.m.

The knocking was part of my dream. Or I thought it was. The part of my mind that was aware of the external world convinced me that if I woke up there wouldn't be any knocking, that I was dreaming the knocking. So why wake up? Just slip back into full sleep; you needed the rest anyway, friend.

But then some part of me figured out that the knocking was real and that it was in fact getting louder and more persistent and that somebody on the other side of my hotel room door was suddenly and sharply calling my name.

I don't know what I did exactly, but without my sling I managed to inflict a whole lot of pain as I slid my legs off the bed. I grabbed my Colt from the holster on the floor and barefooted my way to the door.

It was Marshal Wickham. "Somethin's sure goin' on here, Ford."

"What're you talking about?"

"Get your socks and boots on and I'll tell you."

The first thing I did was get my sling back on and then I tended, one-armed, to my socks and boots.

"That's a bitch, getting boots on one-handed," Wickham said. "I never thought of that before."

"So you're pounding on my door and shouting my name. What the hell's going on?"

"The desk clerk told me that Spenser was here to see you earlier and he looked real scared."

"You woke me up to tell me that?"

"No, I woke you up to tell you that somebody got into Spenser's hotel room and cut his throat. Just the way they cut your brother's throat."

PART THREE

Chapter 16

I spent an hour in Spenser's hotel room. I mostly went through his two travel bags and his mail. He'd apparently been on the road for some time. He had twenty-six pieces of mail. I went through each one, found nothing that bore on the gun or his murder.

Brinkley and Wayland were sitting in Marshal Wickham's front area when we got there.

"Sorry to keep you waiting," Wickham said.

With four of us in there, Wickham's modest office was crowded. Wickham didn't waste any time. He said, "So who's killing you men off?"

Brinkley said, "Why don't you tell us, Marshal? Unless I'm mistaken, that star you wear means that you represent law and order in this hick burg."

Wickham glanced at me. Frowned. People think that when you wear a badge, citizens snap to. A lot of them don't. Given the circumstances, Wickham's question was well taken. But they didn't feel like answering him, so they didn't.

He looked back at them. "Let me put it this way, then. Why would somebody want to kill you four men?"

Brinkley and Wayland looked at each other. Then they faced Wickham and Brinkley said, "The gun. Why the hell else would they kill us?"

"You're telling me you have the gun?" Wickham said.

"No," Wayland said, "he's telling you somebody thinks we have the gun."

"Then you don't?"

"No."

"Any idea who does?"

"No."

"And no idea, of course, who killed Fairbain or Spenser?"

Brinkley spoke: "You're the lawman here, remember? If you don't know, how the hell can you expect us to know?"

Wayland said, "I want to leave town."

"Not quite yet, I'm afraid," Wickham said. "If you're afraid you might be killed, you can always stay here."

"Here, meaning the jail?" Brinkley said. "Why would two respectable businessmen want to be thrown into a jail cell with a bunch of ne'er-do-wells?"

"You're forgetting," I said to Wickham, "these are very high-toned men. Selling arms is an admirable business."

"Why is he here?" Brinkley asked.

"He's a law officer same as I am."

"This is your jurisdiction."

"He's Federal."

Brinkley scowled.

Wickham said, "So you don't know why anybody would want to kill you, even though two of you are dead. You don't have any idea who might be behind the killings. And even though you wouldn't ever consider staying in a cell here where you'd be safe, you want to leave town because you're afraid the killer will take your lives if you don't."

"None of that sounds particularly unreasonable," Brinkley said.

Wayland: "I want to know how much longer we have to stay here."

Wickham was about to speak when I slipped the envelopes from inside my jacket pocket and held them up in the air. "Before you answer that, Marshal, let me ask them if they know anything about these envelopes." There were four of them. Two each. They took them, looked them over. Handed them back.

"Envelopes," Wayland said. "More of a waste of time. Now will you answer my question, Marshal? When can we leave town?"

I said, "Fairbain sent James four of these. James's wife claims that James knew something and that's why Fairbain sent him cashier's checks."

They managed to look conspicuously innocent.

"That's between Fairbain and James," Wayland said.

"And you of course wouldn't know anything about it, either, I suppose?" I said to Brinkley.

"Hell, no, I don't. The only time I ever saw Fairbain was when we were together in town here. Otherwise we didn't keep any contact. I had no idea what he did."

I slid all four of the envelopes into my pocket. "I'll bet you've heard the word 'blackmail' before."

"What's that supposed to mean?" Wayland said.

"Somebody was blackmailing Fairbain," I said.

"So?"

"So, Wayland, maybe you knew why he was being blackmailed. Or maybe the same blackmailer was getting money from you."

"Hardly. And as Brinkley said, I didn't know anything about Fairbain except what he told us when we were together in town here."

"Spenser must have known," I said. "He was killed, too."

"I still don't see what that has to do with us," Wayland said.

I smiled at Wickham. "Have you ever seen such a pair of innocents?"

"Not since I made my First Communion," he said. "The gun they were after gets stolen, two of their cohorts get killed, and at least one of their group looks like he was paying blackmail money. And these two don't know anything about any of it."

"They must sleep a lot," I said.

"An awful lot," Wickham said.

"This is all very funny," Brinkley said, "but it's also a waste of time." He stood up. "Unless you're arresting me, Marshal, I plan to walk out of that door over there right now."

"And the same goes for me," Wayland said. He stood up, too.

"You're not being very smart," Wickham said. "Looks like somebody is after you, but you won't take any help."

"The only help I want is to get on that train and get out of here," Wayland said.

"You could probably sneak on a train or a stage," Wickham said, "and I wouldn't be able to stop you.

But once I found out you were gone, I'd put out an arrest warrant on you. I know a lot about you by now. No matter where you went, I'd find a way to serve that warrant."

"Arrest us for what?" Brinkley said.

I said, "Maybe you two knew something that Fairbain and Spenser did. Maybe you're the blackmailers."

"This is getting stupider by the minute," Brinkley said.

"Is it? I'm sure the marshal will be happy to help me search your rooms. Maybe we'll find something there that'll clear this whole thing up."

I was congratulating myself on how deftly I'd bluffed them when Brinkley said, "I can't speak for Wayland here, but feel free to check my room. In fact, you can go up there now and go through it. Tear it apart for all I care. I'll even wait right here for you to come back and stammer your way through a few excuses for not finding anything."

"Same for me," Wayland said. "You check out my room and I'll sit here and wait for you."

See, it's not supposed to work that way. You're supposed to bluff them and they're supposed to get all nervous and sweaty and give you all kinds of legal reasons why you can't search their rooms and you'd better damned not try.

I'd forgotten that it works the other way sometimes. The bluffer can get outbluffed, too.

"You want to go check out my room or not?" Brinkley said.

I shrugged. "Maybe later."

He smirked. "Your little bluff didn't work so well, did it, Federal man?"

"I guess I'll have to work on it a little more."

" 'Work on it a little more,' " Brinkley sneered.

They sneered at both Wickham and me, in fact, and then left.

You knew the town had come of age when you saw the tiny window bearing the words REAL ESTATE OFFICE. They were repeated on the glass of the door, in case you missed them on the window.

The interior was short and narrow. One wall had framed lithographs of the president, the territorial governor, and a cranky-looking old bastard who probably founded the town. There was a law about that. All town founders had to look like mountain men and look cranky as hell. Of course most town-founder stories are bullshit. But that's the law, too. Who wants to hear the truth when you can hear the myth. Maybe he didn't really hold off six hundred Injuns by himself. But it was better than the truth, hearing that one day he had the trots real bad, stopped off by the river down here, and decided to stay a while. Bloodthirtsy Injuns make for a much better tale.

There were two desks. One was occupied by a gray-haired woman in a blue dress with a high, frilly, white collar. Several of her fingers, working blur fast, inflicted pain on typewriter keys. The keys striking the platen seemed as long as pellet shots in the sun-streaming silence.

The other desk, behind hers, was empty. Behind that desk were three wooden three-door filing cabinets and a large map of the county.

She didn't look up. She didn't even stop assaulting the typewriter. She said, "May I help you?"

"Are you the realtor?"

"I am the realtor's secretary."

"Well, maybe you could help me."

Still typing away.

"Are you looking for land, sir?"

"No. Some information on who owns a certain cabin."

She stopped typing, turned around with great efficiency in her swivel chair. She had a sweet-ugly face, just now showing the loose flesh of age. "Then you would want Mr. Benson."

"Mr. Benson?"

"Mr. Richard Benson. Sole owner and proprietor of Benson Realty."

"Benson Realty. I see. It just says Real Estate on the window."

"Mr. Benson thought of naming the company after himself but he decided it would look vain."

"A humble realtor. I see."

"A humble and successful realtor. There are three realtors in the county. We outsold them four to one last year."

"Maybe he'll have to reconsider putting his name on the door."

She caught the sarcasm. "I'm very busy. And Mr. Benson isn't here and won't be back until tomorrow. He's on a train coming back from Denver."

"And you're sure you can't help me?"

"I'd prefer not to. I told somebody something once that I shouldn't have. It gave another realtor an edge in a deal Mr. Benson was trying to close. Mr. Benson was nice enough not to fire me. But now I'm strictly a secretary. Mr. Benson handles everything else."

"Like your job, huh?" I looked around. It was an orderly place—I suspected this was due to her—with modern office furnishings and a couple of leather-bound books that no doubt contained photos of everything Benson was selling. Plus there was the sweet scent of furniture polish on the air. This was a place where you could relax and think. You didn't have all the traffic of a retail store to keep you on edge with insincere goodwill and people trying to haggle you out of your profit.

"Do you see this?" she was saying.

"The typewriter?"

"Only one of three in the entire county."

"Impressive."

"And the blond filing cabinets? Only First Montana Bank has filing cabinets as modern as these."

I nodded. "Nice."

"And Mr. Benson says that we'll have the first telephone in town. They're putting up the poles and lines now."

She had an owner's pride. She also suddenly had a child's enthusiasm. Her face in that moment was not only sweet-ugly. It was also downright cute.

"I'm sorry I can't help you."

"Oh, that's all right. I don't want to get either one of you in trouble."

She'd been eyeing me closely for the last couple of minutes. Now came the revelation. "You're David's brother."

"That I am."

"He sure was a charmer." Then, not wanting to appear foolish: "And quite the businessman. He got

Mr. Benson to drop his price considerably for that ranch. He made a lot of inquiries before he came here and when Mr. Benson told him the rental price, your brother said he'd pay so much and nothing more. Mr. Benson isn't used to that kind of customer. When I was going to get married again—I'm a widow—I had my eye on a nice little house and even for me Mr. Benson would only go so low."

"So you didn't buy the house?"

"No, and as it turned out we wouldn't have needed it anyway. The marshal found another woman."

"Marshal Wickham?"

She smiled and shook her head. "Don't look so surprised. Old folks have romances, too. He just found somebody else." She looked down at her type-writer and then back at me. "I got over it." But the confidence of the voice didn't match the wistfulness of the gaze.

I waited for Jane in the room where everybody took their breaks. I waited nearly half an hour. When she came in, she looked tired. She picked up the half-empty coffeepot and waggled it at me. I shook my head and slapped my hand over my empty cup; she filled her cup and came over and sat down. We didn't say anything. She blew upward on a stray piece of hair lying across her forehead. That didn't work, so she carefully lifted up the piece of hair and smoothed it back into the rest of her hair.

She started to take a sip of coffee, then stopped. Too hot apparently. She blew on the surface of the black, steaming coffee.

"You all right?"

"Long day. We lost Mr. Hendricks. One of my favorite old men."

"I'm sorry."

"You shouldn't get as attached as I do."

"Better than not getting attached. People generally know when you're concerned for them."

She didn't say anything. Went back to her coffee.

"I came here to ask you a couple of questions."

"The Army investigator."

"That's right."

"I hope my head is clear enough to answer. I need a lot of sleep."

"Hard to sleep?"

"I just lie there and think about your brother."

Pretty damned unseemly when you come right down to it. How I felt hurt every time she mentioned David romantically. She'd been his woman—one of them, anyway—and I sure didn't have any claim on her. But every time she mentioned him I felt like a spurned lover.

Then I brought up the island, which I'd been thinking about more and more.

"He ever say anything about maybe hiding the gun on Parson's Cairn?"

"Not to me, he didn't. But the more I think about the island, the more I remember him talking about it. He liked it over there. Said he could sit there and finally get some thinking done."

"He mention what he was thinking about?"

A half-laugh. "I always wanted him to say that he was thinking about me. About us. But he never did."

"He ever take you there?"

"Huh-uh. I was kind of a stick-in-the-mud, I'm

afraid. I wasn't all that keen on going to the island. All those bugs and quicksand."

"He ever talk about the hunting cabin there?"

"Oh, yes. Talked it up quite a bit. How comfortable I'd be in it."

"He ever mention any trouble in the cabin?"

"Trouble?" She watched my face. "I'm not sure what you mean."

She wanted any scrap of information I could find about him. The more information, the more alive he was in her mind. I told her about the cabin and the blood on the floor.

"Did it look like fresh blood?"

"I don't think so. Pretty old, in fact."

"He never mentioned having any trouble there. A lot of different people rented it out for hunting."

"Yeah, I want to talk to this realtor about the renter list."

"Dick Benson?"

"Uh-huh."

She laughed cordially. "He's actually a very charitable man. But he'd double-charge his own mother for a pup tent. He's like a drummer in that respect, I suppose. He hates to leave without selling you something—and just about anything'll do."

The wall clock fixed her attention. "I've got an hour to go on my shift. I need to start working again."

Sitting there in the sunlight, worn out from work and missing my brother, I knew he would have moved on to another woman soon enough. When you looked at her closely, you saw signs of the worst disease of all—at least to David it had been the worst disease—getting older. I'd figured out long ago that men who constantly need to be around younger and younger women are around them in hopes of denying their own impending old age. How old can I be if I still attract young women? They can get away with it for a time, but then they start looking foolish; and ultimately they look sort of sinister.

I wanted to touch her hand, and for once not out of some stupid sense of romance. She'd be a long time getting over David and by then I'd be long gone. I just wanted the touch to say that she was a good woman and that I felt bad about her grief but that her goodness would get her through it.

But I didn't touch her hand, of course. She would've taken it the wrong way and things were complicated enough.

She walked me to the corridor and then down to the front door. "Just be careful," she said lightly. "Dick Benson's got these old monstrosities he's been trying to unload for years. Everybody who lives here just walks away when he starts his spiel. But he considers strangers prime targets."

"I'll be careful. After I get the information I'll gag him."

"It's about time somebody did."

I drank three cups of coffee and then went for a walk along the river, through the small town park, and then stopped in at the café for some eggs and flapjacks. Nothing tastes better than an afternoon breakfast.

I was just finishing up when Wayland came through the door. He was still wearing that big, new, stupid hat of his. His gaze searched for something, and when it lit on me, he made one of those big surprised looks that stage actors favor.

He came over and sat himself down.

"Did you know that James's wife Gwen has a lover?"

Every once in a while you get shocked. It doesn't even have to be true, what somebody tells you. Just the idea of it—even if you scorn it later on as bullshit—just the idea of something your mind finds offensive can shock you. And even the most cynical person in this old vale of tears can be told something that absolutely stuns him.

"Yeah, and General Grant could fly."

"You don't understand what I'm saying here."

"Sure, I do. And that's why I know it's bullshit."

"You're seeing her as you want to see her. The sweet, faithful wife."

"Is this supposed to have some bearing on the murders and the gun?"

"It will once I tell you who her lover is."

"Do I win anything if I guess right?"

"Frank Clarion's been slipping it to her for more than a year."

"The deputy? Wickham's nephew?"

"The one and only. So think about it. James tells his good and faithful wife that he and Tib are going to the ranch to help you bring your brother in. But Frank goes out there first, kills your brother, and then guns down James and Tib."

"So why would he kill Fairbain and Spenser?"

"You're not as smart as I thought you were, Ford." He said this smugly. "You should be way ahead of me on this. He goes to Fairbain and offers him the gun. But Fairbain won't meet the price. So now he has to kill Fairbain because Fairbain can fink him out. Then he goes to Spenser. Same thing. He wants

too much money and Spenser says no. He kills
Spenser. He has to. But who would suspect him?
Everybody sees him as this good man doing his job.
But just wait about six months or so when this
thing's blown over. His wife's going to have a little
accident. Maybe drowning. Or maybe a fire. Hell,
maybe it'll be his wife and kid. Man kills as easily as
he has, he could kill his own kid, too. I'm told killing
gets into your blood. But then you'd know all about
that, wouldn't you, Ford? You killed quite a few
Rebs during the war. And my understanding is that
you still kill people when old Uncle Sam deems it
necessary." He paused. Took a drink of water. "So
now Clarion and James's widow are in the clear.
They court for a while and then decide to leave town.
By this time, Clarion has sold the gun and has plenty
of cash for settling down somewhere else. And nobody around here thinks anything more about it.
Everybody's moved on mentally—there's plenty of
things to worry about besides some murder in the
past."

"That's quite a story." By now, it was pretty clear
what he was doing—giving me something so I'd give
him something.

"If you won't go after him, I will."

I ordered a fresh cup of coffee and while I waited
for it I rolled a cigarette. After I got my coffee, I said,
"Where'd you get all this information?"

"Tib's wife."

"Why'd she talk to you?"

"She didn't want to. Not at first. But then I told
her about Tib coming to see me."

"When was this?"

"Three, four hours before he left for the ranch

with you. He asked me how much I'd pay if he double-crossed you and James and got the gun."

"How was he going to get us out of the way?"

"Kill you. Then blame it on the crossfire. He probably could've pulled it off, too."

"And Tib's wife told you about Clarion and Gwen Andrews, too?"

"Sure. Tib told her all about it—about them carrying on together with James not knowing anything about it."

I had to let it settle inside me. That's the trouble with gossip. You might say bullshit right off the top—and it might indeed be bullshit—but it takes root inside you. Even if it's proved false to your satisfaction later on, it's there, in you, in the air. A lot of reputations have been destroyed that way, false rumors; and a lot more will be.

"I can't see it."

"You could if you'd look beyond that saintly role she plays."

"She loved James."

"She said she did, anyway."

"You shoulda been an elixir salesman, Wayland. You got the tongue for it."

"I'm just saying what's in the air. You have respect for women. You believe them. So do I. Most of the time. But every once in a while you run across one who doesn't deserve that pedestal you put them on. And that's the case here, my friend. Whether you want to believe it or not. Now if you want the gun, and I know you do; and if you want the people who killed your brother, and I know you do—you'll throw in with me."

I laughed. "You going to shoot me or stab me?"

"What?"

"Say it's true. Say Frank Clarion and Gwen did kill my brother and take the gun."

"And killed Fairbain and Spenser."

"All right, let's throw that in the pot, too. Killed James and Tib and my brother; killed Fairbain and Spenser. Let's assume that's all true. So we go after Clarion and Gwen."

"And the gun."

"All right, and the gun."

"Now that sounds pretty good to me."

"I'm sure it does, Wayland. Because you're already figuring on killing me."

"Like hell I am."

"How else you going to get the gun?"

He blushed, actually blushed. He'd been trapped. "I thought maybe you'd reconsider and make that deal I proposed."

"No, you didn't. You know I want to take the gun back to Washington, where it belongs. You also know that I may not be the smartest and toughest investigator the Army has, but one thing I am is honest. No matter what you offered me, I wouldn't take it. And that would leave you only one option. You'd have to kill me, Wayland, in order to get that gun you wanted."

"I don't go around shooting people."

"Not unless you need to."

He put on a little show for me. The outraged citizen. "I come to you with the story of what's really going on here—the name of the man who killed your brother, for God's sake—and this is what I get?"

"This is what you get."

He lifted his ten-gallon hat from the table. "I

deeply resent this, sir." He was on the stage again, ham actor.

We exchanged one of those glares that are supposed to strike the other man dead. But both of us survived. He left the café. I sat there and finished my coffee.

Chapter 17

I sat my horse in the woods that ran behind James's house. My field glasses told me that Gwen and her daughter were gone. I'd been here quite a while and hadn't seen anybody. They were in town, maybe.

What I wanted to do was disprove Wayland's story about Gwen and Frank Clarion. It wasn't so much that I had great faith in women—neither sex has any real corner on morality, though women strike me as a lot more reasonable to deal with in general—it was just the simple notion that Gwen would ever take up with Frank Clarion. I needed evidence to disprove Wayland's wild tale—or evidence to prove it.

I gave myself ten minutes. I slipped from my horse, crossed the wide lawn separating house from woods, and eased myself in the back door. Cooking smells, beef and bread. A doll in a gingham dress and blond hair sitting upright in the middle of the kitchen, enormous blue eyes holding secrets I'd never be able to guess. I moved quickly to the other rooms. I had no idea what I was looking for. Maybe the kind of proof I needed didn't even exist. It was doubtful they'd written each other letters that laid out their whole relationship—if they'd ever had one.

James had pretty much given up his Cree heritage, at least judging by the things I found in the house. There were a few ceremonial weapons, a clay pipe for smoking, a pair of moccasins decorated with hand-drawn symbols I took to be Cree, and a tribal headdress heavy enough to snap the neck of the poor sonofabitch who had to wear it for long.

There was much more evidence of the little girl. Books, games, blankets with her name embroidered on them, a hobby horse with mismatched buttons for eyes.

Gwen had three dresses, all worn from wearing, half a dozen shirts, and riding skirt and blouse. On the table next to the bed were three Louisa May Alcott novels.

There was a small desk, two tables with drawers, and the sort of long, metal box used for storing valuables to look through. Nothing especially interesting in any of them.

The soughing wind hid their sounds at first. I didn't really hear them until Julia's voice sailed right through the back window and into the living room where I stood. It's always a bit awkward to have folks walk in and find you looking through their things. Most of the time they look surprised, and then they look betrayed. It'd be better if they looked mad. That'd be much easier to handle than the betrayed look. Much easier.

Gwen went through the whole range—surprise,

shock, anger, betrayal. She did it in just a few seconds, too. Julia was less abstract: "How come he's in our house, Mommy?"

Gwen's eyes showed fury again. "Maybe he'll be nice enough to explain that, honey."

"Look, I was just . . ."

I glanced desperately from Julia to her. "Honey," Gwen said, taking Julia's little hand and turning her toward the back door. "Why don't you go play outside?"

"What should I play, Mommy?"

"Well, how about playing with the new kittens?"

"I did that this morning."

"Well, how about playing with your new ball?"

"I did that this morning, too."

Gwen glanced over her shoulder at me. A faint impression of exasperation was in her eyes. I had to wonder if I'd ever have enough patience to be a parent.

Gwen turned back to Julia and said, "I know. Have you ever rolled the ball past the kittens and had them chase it?"

"I guess not."

"That'd be fun for both you and the kittens, don't you think?"

"I guess so. I'm sort of sleepy, though." For emphasis, she rubbed her right eye.

"Well, you go play for a little while, then I'll make you some warm milk and we'll take a nap. All right?"

"I guess so," Julia said, still sounding reluctant.

Gwen scooted the kid away and when she heard the back door slam, she turned around again with a fistful of surprise. She pointed a Colt .45 directly at my chest.

"I'm guessing you heard about Frank and me."

Hard to guess which was the bigger surprise. The gun or the somewhat casual way she brought up Clarion.

Before I could say anything, she went on quickly. "Nobody knew how James treated me. I tried to leave several times. He said he'd track me down if I did. He wouldn't kill me, he said. He'd kill Julia. I didn't have any doubt he'd do just that, either. You had to know him. How crazy he was. Frank Clarion came out here a couple of times when James was drunk. He stopped James from hurting me. I didn't expect anything to start. In fact, I thought Frank was pretty much of a fool in some ways."

She walked over and sat down in a rocking chair.

"I can see where holding that gun up would make you tired," I said. "Why don't you set it down?"

"It's not the gun that's making me tired. It's my monthly visitor, in case you're interested. It always tires me out."

"If you get to sit, how about me sitting?"

"I didn't know Frank was going to kill James. He never told me that."

"I'll take that as a yes," I said, and sat down in a chair of my own.

"I didn't know he was going to kill anybody, in fact. I only told him about James helping you out because I thought that maybe he could steal the gun from you—after you got it from your brother. That's how I thought he was going to handle it."

"So he gets the gun and then what?"

She let her gaze drop for a moment. Regret made her lean face even sharper. "We run away together."

"He has a wife and kid."

"Figure it out, Ford. We were in love. Or thought we were. We were very selfish people. We didn't worry about husbands or wives or even children. He only agreed to let me take Julia along because I convinced him that James would kill her otherwise."

"You're still running away?"

She snorted. "After he killed all those people? He's not right. Up here." She tapped her head. "He's even crazier than James was. I have to have this gun on me at all times. I sleep with it on the night table. He's mad because I won't take off with him now. He thinks he can sell the gun in New Orleans. He says there's a hotel where all the arms merchants hang out there."

"The La Pierre."

"I guess. Anyway, he claims I've destroyed his life." The snort again. "I've destroyed his life? After he killed all those people. That's the only reason Tib's wife won't go to the marshal. She knows that Frank'll kill her if she does. That he'll find some way. Frank's a very devious man."

The first bullet shattered the west window. The second bullet shattered an oil lamp, which exploded, sending a fist-sized ball of flame along the top of the horsehair couch.

Out back, Julia screamed.

After the first bullet, Gwen had crouched down and headed for the back door. There was no point in trying to stop her. She was out to save her child. There's no more profound urge than that.

I crawled to the side of the west window to get a

fix on where he was. I smashed out what was left of the glass and took a two-second scan of the land. He was out near the barn.

The next minute—and it seemed much longer than that—unfolded this way: Frank Clarion had apparently not been aware of Julia—who'd been on the other side of the barn—until she screamed. Her screams had obviously gotten his attention. Now she was running toward the house. Clarion made the decision to go after her.

Just then Gwen slammed out of the back door and started running toward her daughter. Sight of Gwen must have made Clarion lose control. He shot Gwen twice.

I wanted to fire, but I couldn't. All three of them were now in range, but they'd also collected together in the middle of the backyard. Gwen was crying out and falling in such a way that she obscured Julia and that gave Clarion time to grab Julia.

By the time Gwen's body collided with the unyielding ground, Frank Clarion had what he wanted: a hostage.

"I have to tell you to drop your gun?"

"I guess not."

"Then do it."

"What's he going to do to me?" Julia asked me, her lower lip trembling so badly I could barely understand her. Then, as if realizing everything that had happened in the past few minutes, she looked to her left and saw the fallen form of her mother, who lay unmoving facedown on the ground. "Mom!" she cried and suddenly tried to tear herself from Clarion's armlock around her neck. She kicked him in the shin. For the space of a breath, his hold loosened. I had the exhilarating sense that she was going to jerk and twist free of him. But then his grip was redoubled and when she tried to kick him again, he clipped her on top of the head with the handle of his gun. She slumped in his arm, awake but in pain.

He was done now. Didn't matter if he had a hostage; didn't matter if he had David's gun. He had to know that his world was caving in on him. The shame of destroying his marriage, the shame of murdering several men, and finally the shame of having to take a little girl hostage to save himself—in his frenzy he had to give up on his dime-novel dream of himself. He wasn't the good guy, he was the bad guy. In his case, a very bad guy.

As if to mock us with its indifference, the cacophony of day went right on its way. Birds sang, sweet breezes blew, cows did what cows do, and the wee kittens were cute and playful. Who gave a damn about this stupid human drama where a little girl was probably about to lose her life? Humans were always doing stupid things like this. They never changed, never learned. Birds, cows and wee kittens had given up on humans a long time ago, anyway.

"I'm walking her to my horse. I don't have to tell you what happens if you make a move on me, Ford."

"You killed too many people, Clarion. You'll never walk away."

"You don't have no idea what's really going on around here."

"What about James and Tib—and my brother?"

Julia started to rouse. She'd hung limply in his arms but now, like a puppet whose strings had been reattached, the limbs got awkwardly active, jutting this way and that for the arms, the knees strong enough to force the legs to stand upright.

"I didn't kill nobody. The way I figure, it was Wayland. He heard me run my mouth off to Tib one night when we were drinking—how I was going to kill your brother and take the gun for myself. That was my plan. But by the time I got there, they were all dead. And somebody was in the barn, firing at you and James and Tib. I just rode back to town. Now put your arms up in the air."

His bay was west of the house, ground-tied. He wouldn't have any trouble reaching it. Julia was crying quietly, glancing at her mother every few minutes.

Nothing I could do. He was going to leave and he knew there wasn't a damn thing I could do about it. Julia tried kicking him again, but this time he moved his leg out of the way in time. He slugged her again on the side of the head, but not as hard as last time.

"Is my mommy dead, mister?" she cried out at me as Frank Clarion dragged her past me to his horse.

"She'll be all right, honey."

Clarion laughed. "You shoulda been a priest, Ford."

Julia started crying again. At that moment the world couldn't make much sense to her. If it ever would again. Far as I could tell, her mother was dead.

He got around the house. He wasn't having any trouble with Julia. She'd either given up or had passed out. Her arms dangled at her sides, seeming to swing free. I heard a horse whinny and then I heard Clarion muttering instructions to Julia. He was setting her up on his saddle. He was telling her he'd shoot her if she didn't sit absolutely still. The silence was such that I could hear his saddle leather when he climbed up on the horse. The horse whinnied again and moved around some. He settled it down before moving it away from the yard. He started out slow, the horse moving just a few yards. I wondered if he was having trouble with Julia. Strange he didn't just start moving fast. A second or two before he did it, I figured out why he was moving so slow. There was one shot and then a second. I don't know how to describe the sound my horse made, a cry that was part shock and part pain. Then the sound became pure pain. The horse collapsed. The sound seemed as enormous as the cry of pain had been. Then Clarion was moving fast and so was I.

The horse was dead by the time I got to it. Tremors skittered across its flesh like spiderflies on a pond surface. At least the prick had been merciful. Two bullets in the brain.

Gwen was stone dead. You could feel the life still warm but cooling fast in the horse. But Gwen was cold dead. I turned her over on her back. Black ants had collected on the blood red of her blouse. She'd hit the ground so hard that her sharp prairie-elegant nose had been smashed. She smelled pretty bad, everything having emptied out the way it did. People didn't figure sometimes, didn't figure at all, and she was one of them. Whatever James had done to her, a shitkicker thief like Clarion sure wasn't the solution.

Clarion had forgotten about the horse out back of the barn, the one Gwen used for her buckboard. I remembered it only because it made some noise on the downwind. I dragged my saddle off my own poor, dead animal and got it on the ancient cutting horse that somebody had returned from the cattle business years earlier. Getting it to stand still while I saddled it was no easy task. When I finally grabbed the horn and started to swing myself up into the saddle, it spooked and nearly threw me to the ground.

It took me ninety-two minutes by railroad watch to reach town. It should have taken me sixty at the outside.

Chapter 18

Marshal Wickham was in his office. Just inside the front door, I could hear him talking back there. I didn't wait for somebody to find me and escort me back.

His door was closed. I opened it and put my head in.

He was talking to a man in muttonchops. The disgusted way the man looked at me said that he was important. His two big ruby rings and his expensive purple suit said he was important, too. I'm sure he was the president of a lodge or two.

"In case you hadn't noticed," Wickham said, "I'm sort of busy at the moment." He sounded mad and I didn't blame him.

I said, "I want you to swear out a warrant for Clarion on one count of murder. There may be others later on."

Muttonchops turned in his chair and said, "Who the hell is this man, anyway?"

But I'd obviously gotten Wickham's attention. "What the hell are you talking about, Ford?"

"He just killed Gwen and kidnapped her daughter."

"Frank Clarion? My deputy?" Easy to see that he

wasn't beyond shock, either, not even for all his years as a lawman. "That's my nephew."

He was talking gibberish, the way we all do when we don't know what else to say. As if it was impossible for his nephew to be capable of even the smallest crime.

"He grew up right here in town."

"I certainly hope you know what the hell you're talking about," Muttonchops said.

I said, "You need to get out of here." I grabbed him under his hefty arm and jerked him to his feet.

"Just who the hell do you think you are?" he snapped.

"He's Federal, Felix. Maybe you'd better leave."

"I don't give a damn if he's Federal or not. I don't like being treated this way."

I tried to make it easier for him. "You're right. I shouldn't have treated you like this. But it's an emergency and the marshal here and I need to get to work."

He was calmed, but not by much. "Federal or not doesn't give you a right to treat one of the most prominent men in this whole Territory the way you just did."

"You're right, it doesn't, sir."

"Go on now, Felix. I'll explain this all later."

Muttonchops picked up his bowler. Flicked fat fingers at dust I couldn't see. "You haven't had any bigger supporter than me over the years, Marshal. I'd keep that in mind."

He walked out. He tried to look dignified but he tended to waddle and waddling is a bitch when it comes to dignity.

I closed the door.

Wickham said, "You better be on the money with this, Ford. That man is the biggest gossip in three states. My nephew's reputation'll be ruined within half an hour."

"He's already ruined it himself," I said.

"Let's hear it then."

He sat down. Grabbed his pipe. The ruddy face was suddenly pale. "What the hell am I going to tell my sister if this is true? He was a kind of rough-and-tumble kid, but he never got into any serious trouble before."

"Any deputies here?"

"Two in the back, one going off shift, another coming on."

"Tell them to go round up Wayland and Brinkley."

"For what?"

"Now," I said. "Right now. I'm pulling rank on you, Marshal."

He went and started talking to them in a loud, harassed voice. He told them to each take a repeater, because he didn't know what they were walking into, the fucking Federale not telling him a fucking thing, so take the fucking repeaters, you hear me?

Then he came back and slammed the door shut behind him and went and sat behind his desk and said, "I didn't like you much before, Ford. Now I don't even like you that much."

I told him everything I knew and when I finished, he said, "Now there's a load of horseshit if I ever heard it. I can't believe he's a killer."

"He killed Gwen, if nobody else."

"If you say so." He was bitter.

It was clear he couldn't admit this to himself. He could convince me that Clarion couldn't have done all it took to kill people and get the gun. But he couldn't convince me he hadn't killed Gwen. He couldn't convince me because I'd been there and seen it.

Then, "He kill her in cold blood?"

"Second degree. They won't hang him."

There were tears in his voice. "And I'll have to go tell his mother. My sister's a damned sweet woman and her health isn't all that good, anyway. I'm just afraid of what this'll do to her."

"I'm sorry for that, Marshal. But right now I'm worried about little Julia. How fast can you round up a posse?"

His eyes were distant. I supposed he was rehearsing his words to his sister. Seems like our Frank kind've went a little crazy, I'm afraid, Sis. He, uh. Killed a woman and now he's kidnapped a little girl. I hate to say this, Sis, but if he contacts you in any way, you'll have to let me know right away. It'll be better if we bring him in safe and sound. I've got a posse looking for him and if they find him first— well, every lawman, even a young one like Frank, he makes enemies in a town this size. And I'm sure there are a couple of fellas who'd just love to shoot him. Now, don't cry, honey. I'm not tryin' to scare you; I'm just trying to make you understand that you and I have to do everything we can to bring him in safe and sound. I know how loyal you are to him—but right now you need to help me bring him in.

Then, coming out of his thoughts, he said, "What'd you say?"

"I said we need a posse, and damned fast."

"That won't be any trouble."

He usually stood up fast and straight, the way a

much younger man would. But there was a decided weariness in his bones and posture now. He looked his age. "I'll need half an hour."

"I'll be out front."

The men were about what you'd expect to find in a town this size. Six of the men were middle-aged, sober, quiet. They wore heavy coats and carried hunting rifles.

You can usually judge a posse by its demeanor. The two young men passed a pint of rye back and forth and laughed a lot.

I walked up to the one with the fancy Stetson and said, "We won't be needing you boys."

"Oh, is that right? And just who the fuck would you be?"

I showed them my badge. "Appreciate you stopping by. But these six men'll be all we need."

His friend with the flat-brimmed black hat said, "You can't tell us what to do."

"I can as far as this posse's concerned. Now, again, I appreciate you stopping by. Maybe we can use you later on, but for now, we've got what we need."

I didn't realize just how drunk they were until Stetson started for his gun. He caught his thumb on his belt loop. I ripped the gun from his holster and pointed it at him and told him to get down.

"You ain't got no right to order me around."

"Sure, I do," I said. Then lost patience. I reached

up and grabbed the edge of his sheepskin and jerked him out of his saddle and stirrups. He hit the ground hard, the way a drunk usually does. Somebody shouted, "Behind you!"

I swiveled in time to see his friend going for his gun. Stetson had been drunk and clumsy. This one was drunk and slow. I put a bullet in his hat and said, "The next one goes into your forehead."

Wickham had been inside, giving one of his day deputies instructions for holding down the office while the boss was gone.

The marshal was preceded out the front door by the barrel of his Winchester. "What the hell's goin' on out here?"

"These two," I said. "I want them jugged for twenty-four hours."

"Verne," he said, over his shoulder. "Get out here and bring your shotgun." He sneered at the two young ones. "The Link brothers. I thought I told you, you weren't invited on this posse."

"It's a free country," said the one just picking himself up from the ground. He still looked dazed from hitting the ground so hard.

The other one said, petulantly, "He darned near killed me, Marshal. And with no call at all."

"Phil was goin' for his gun," one of the older posse men said. "Behind this man's back."

"Gosh, Phil," the marshal said, "and here I figured you were innocent as usual. People just like to shoot at you for no reason at all, don't they?"

"You don't have no call to mock me," Phil said.

Wickham scowled. "Punks with pride." He nodded to Verne. "Get them the hell in a cell."

Verne came and led the Link brothers off.

Wickham spent five minutes dividing the six men into two groups, giving them specific areas to cover. Then we were off. Wickham and I rode together.

It was three hours before we found Frank Clarion. The chill told me that despite the sunshine and the burning leaves, this was the last of autumn. You could smell and taste the snow that was in the mountains and headed down the passes. Scarecrows watched us from just about half the farm fields; huge orange pumpkins were lined up in front yards, just waiting to be carved into boogeymen; and sleek black crows walked around with a certain jaunty air.

Wickham had written down a list of six places Clarion was likely to hide out. An abandoned railroad shack near the foothills, a cave that the Cree sometimes used for ceremonies, a cave in a limestone wall above a leg in the river, a deserted farmhouse, a burned-out church with a usable basement, and one of Clarion's aunts who loved the boy very much. Too much, according to Wickham.

The burned-out church and the deserted farmhouse were ours. We didn't find him or any evidence that he'd been there. On the stage road back toward town, one of the posse men came riding hard to tell us that everybody was up at the abandoned railroad shack.

We joined the rider for the hour-long journey to the shack. The men were gathered behind a copse of birches, their shotguns leaning against the trees.

"Wanted to wait for you, Marshal," said a man who'd introduced himself to me as Brian Lamott.

"We didn't want to take no chances with that little girl."

"I appreciate that. So you got a look at him?"

Lamott nodded. He must've ground-tied his horse up there in the grass on that hill where we couldn't see it at first. But then the horse drifted down and Pop there saw it and we knew he was here."

The shack was tiny, weather-raw. No windows. I thought of Julia. Her mother dead and her in the control of a scared and crazed young outlaw.

Wickham said, "I'm going to walk over to the shack."

I grabbed his arm. "You sure about this?"

He just looked at me. "This is what you'd do if he was your kin, wouldn't you?"

He knew the answer to that.

"I'll keep a repeater on that door," I said.

"No need. If he wants to kill his own uncle, then I wouldn't want to live, anyway." The weariness in the voice and eyes was now joined with real sadness.

So the seven of us sat and waited and watched. Seven unremarkable men on a tiny piece of unremarkable land playing out a drama that very few people gave a damn about. You had to wonder how many hundreds of such dramas had been played out in the shadow of these looming mountains.

"He won't shoot him," one man said.

"I never did like that little prick," said another.

"I don't hear the little girl cryin' out or nothing," said a third. "Maybe he killed her already."

"Hell of a thing after the way the marshal treated him all these years."

"How about his mama? She don't have good health as it is. Think what'll happen now."

I said nothing. There was nothing to say. I was a stranger here on a job, passing through. I didn't know the particulars of any of it.

Wickham was halfway to the cabin when Clarion ducked into the doorframe and blazed off two quick shots. He didn't hit Wickham, hadn't intended to. He just hoped to scare his uncle. But if his uncle was scared, he didn't show it. He didn't even break step. He just kept walking.

I'd had my repeater trained on the door, but I realized that if a shot went wide it might hit the little girl. And it might just go wide, too, what with the wind. The wood of the shack was so worn a bullet would pass clean through it.

"I want to help you, boy," Wickham shouted. The wind was up. Hard to be heard without shouting.

"Nothin' you can do," Clarion shouted back.

"Is Julia alive?"

"I didn't mean to kill Gwen. I loved her."

"Dammit, I said is the girl alive?"

"Yes. I got her gagged is all."

"I'm coming in."

"I don't want you to do that."

All this time Wickham kept his pace, walking, walking, straight to the shack.

"I'm walking in there, Frank. You'll have to kill me to stop me."

"You sonofabitch."

Which meant that he didn't have whatever he needed—the wrong kind of courage, the right kind of hatred—to kill his own blood.

Just as he reached the cabin, Wickham turned around and cupped a hand to his mouth and said, "You boys go on back to town. I'm gonna handle this myself from now on. I appreciate the help and I'll stand you all to a good meal and a night of drinks. But you head back now."

One thing about Wickham. He had the kind of authority that made whatever he said believable. This wasn't any ruse, any game. He wanted us gone. God alone knew what he had in mind.

The men responded as I figured they would.

"He means it, fellas," one man said.

The others grumbled their agreement.

But it was easy to see they had enough respect for Wickham to do what he said.

"I guess it's a family matter now," a man said.

The retreat was ragged. A couple men didn't mount up till the others had started away. They watched me. "You going?" said the white-haired man.

"You better do what Wickham says," I said.

He said, "Your shit don't stink, huh?"

"He don't gotta go, Fred. He's got a badge."

"So does my grandson. I got it for him for his birthday."

They got on their horses and rode away. I hid behind a boulder. I could hear them in there, their voices but not their words.

I spent most of my time trying to figure out if Wayland had gotten out of town before the deputy got him. He seemed to have a way of finding out things faster than just about anybody. He couldn't leave on a train because the deputy would check that. He couldn't rent a horse and wagon because the livery man would tell us. But what he could do was buy a horse and wagon from a private citizen, pay the man enough to keep his mouth shut, and then take off across country with the gun in the wagon bed and his mind filled with dancing dollar signs.

I thought of David then, and my folks. Sometimes I got sentimental and thought about going back there. But even if I wanted to make it up with them, my presence there would shame them. They probably didn't even speak of me anymore, as if I'd died or had never existed in the first place. A well-raised boy like me fighting on the side of the Union. It was not anything that could ever be lived down. Not for my parents. Society, no matter what society you care to name, never has room for people who betray its most sacred principles, even if those principles are clearly wrong.

The girl came out first. She didn't run. In fact, she moved so slowly I guessed that she was still in some kind of shock. She stumbled a couple of times, but didn't fall. Then right in the middle of the clearing, between my position and the shack, she sat down, probably on Wickham's orders. The two men were still talking inside the cabin. Their voices had raised.

I walked out into the clearing and picked up Julia. Her eyes had the eerie blankness you saw in children of the war. I'd once shot a slaver who was holding three Yankee prisoners. I'd faced him off and told him to turn them over to me. He'd refused and then his son, in the haymow, had leaned out into the sunlight, his rifle barrel glinting. I killed the father first and then the son. A little girl came running out from the back door. She ran straight to the bodies. Her mother came then, trying to comfort the girl. When the girl looked up at me, the emptiness of her gaze startled me. No hatred; not even anger. Just this strange, flat stare. There are some realities the mind doesn't want to register. Julia looked like that now.

There were two shots inside the shack. If my ear was true, two shots from the same gun. Julia started to cry quietly. The sound of the gunshots had probably brought everything back to her, especially the death of her mother. I said, "I'll be right back."

She just stared at me.

But I didn't have to walk far. Wickham came out from the shack. His Colt hung precariously from his fingers, as if he didn't want it. And apparently he didn't, because he let it drop to the ground. Then he just fell back against the shack. The entire structure swayed on the edge of collapse. He wasn't a small man, Wickham.

"What the hell am I going to tell my sister Emma?" he said when I reached him.

He staggered forward, as if he might fall face-down. I got a shoulder against him and said, "Take it easy."

"I didn't have any choice." Tears shook his voice. "He was going to shoot me."

"C'mon, we need to get back to town."

In the middle distance, Julia stood up. Sunlight gleamed on top of her head. Sight of her seemed to make him forget Clarion a moment.

"You go on to her," I said. "I'll get a look at Clarion."

"At Clarion? What the hell for?"

"Make sure he's actually dead, for one thing."

"Oh." He settled down.

"Then I'll get his horse and pitch him over it."

"My poor sister."

"You go on now, Marshal. That little girl could use a friend about now."

He nodded groggily, as if he was only understanding about half of what I said to him.

Chapter 19

I went inside the shack. The dirt floor smelled like an old grave. The other smell gave the impression that every animal within a radius of fifty miles had used this shack as a toilet at one time or another. On top of these smells were the smells Clarion made. He was dead, all right. I didn't need a pulse or a mirror beneath his nose to tell me that. He was dead, all right.

Ten minutes later, I slung him across the back of his horse, tied him down as good as I could, and then I rode back to where Julia and Wickham waited on his horse. She was talking some now. Her eyes shone with life again. A pained expression, true. But life, real life.

The trip back seemed endless. Julia would get crying so hard that we'd have to stop and take turns holding, almost rocking, her like a little baby. She kept asking if her mom was still alive, as if asking it enough times would change the same whispered answer we always gave her.

The men from the posse were in the marshal's office. He went in there and talked to them and I took Julia over to the hospital.

The first thing Jane did was get her two cookies and a glass of milk. We sat at one of the tables in the break room. Julia said she wasn't hungry. She was still young enough to fit nicely on Jane's lap. Jane rocked her and talked to her and suggested that Julia at least try the cookie. She did. She looked ashamed for liking it. How could you eat a cookie when your mother had just been shot to death? But then, like a tiny animal, her small, pale hand darted out at the saucer with the cookie on it and she took another bite.

When I walked into Wickham's private office, he was pulled up tight to his desk. His head was in his hand. He stared straight down at the shiny, empty surface of his desk.

I sat down. "You talk to your sister?"

"Yeah." Not looking up.

"How'd it go?"

"How'd you think it'd go?"

I said nothing. There was nothing to say.

He said, "You should've heard her cry. She lost a five-year-old once, mule kicked the little boy in the back of the head. She didn't cry as much then as she did today. She sounded crazy today." He looked up. His eyes were red. He face was old in an ugly way. "Really crazy."

"You did what you had to."

"She kept saying I could've handled it better."

"People always say that. They can't help saying it any more than you could help doing what you did. It's shitty for everybody involved all the way around."

He needed somebody to take it out on. He said, "It's probably different for you. Washington pays you to kill people. Probably doesn't bother you."

"Probably doesn't."

"I ever tell you I think you're a cold, dishonest asshole?"

"Not quite in those terms, Marshal. But I got the point."

"I killed my own fucking nephew."

He brought down a huge hand with Biblical wrath. I expected to see the desk be cleaved in half.

He scowled at me. "You think you could whip me?"

"Your sister went crazy. That's enough for one family."

"That supposed to be funny, you sonofabitch?"

By the time he finished saying it, he was up on his feet and coming around the desk, starting to charge me.

"That supposed to be funny, I said?" Bellering.

He was too far away to swing, but he swung anyway. I felt sorry for him, but he was tough enough that he could inflict some damage.

I took two quick steps toward him and threw a hard right to his gut and then an equally hard left to his jaw.

He looked betrayed. It was almost funny. He could've looked mad or surprised or physically hurt. But for that first long instant when time froze, just then he looked as if the only friend he'd ever had had betrayed him in a way that never would, or never could, be forgiven.

Then he turned around, staggered back to his desk, and started puking in the wastebasket.

I went up front and talked to Bob Lindsey, the night deputy. "Anybody ever find Wayland and Brinkley?"

"Not yet, I'm afraid. There's a good chance they left town. They're still looking. That's why Wickham pulled me in early. So I could watch the desk here while they looked." His head jerked toward the office in back. "He kill Clarion?"

"Yeah."

"About time somebody did."

"Didn't like him, huh?"

He leaned forward so he could stage-whisper and be heard. "He'd cover things up for money. Wickham's a smart old bird and knew what Frank was doing. But what with his sister and all, Wickham pretended he didn't know what Frank was up to."

"He cover up serious things?"

"He did if you consider murder serious." Then: "You're pretty good with that."

I was rolling a cigarette one-handed. "Tell me about the murder."

"Something happened out to this cabin that tourists use for hunting."

The cabin floor. The bloodstains. I knew instinctively he was talking about the place.

"Richard Benson, he came in here one night all upset and wanting to see the marshal. Told him he was taking his meal. The marshal used to eat at home; then when he was seeing the Cree woman Louise, he'd always meet her at the café for supper. Now he just eats there alone. I asked Benson if I could help him. He said no. Then, just as he was going out, Frank comes in. Benson starts yelling all over again. Then Frank invites him up the street for a beer. I always had the sense that something happened because they found Louise dead not long after and the way I get it there was blood on the cabin floor. I can't say for sure that the two tied together but I do know that Louise's inquest was kind of rushed through and that her death was ruled an accident.

"The marshal wasn't himself for a long time. He'll come out and joke with you a lot of the time. But not then. And every once in a while he'd get into these long arguments with Frank. In his office. With the door closed. The deputies could never figure out what they were arguing about exactly. But one day the marshal give Frank one hell of a shiner, I know that much."

The door opened. A middle-aged woman came in and said, "They ran through my flowers again tonight, Deputy." Gingham dress, matching bonnet; broad, stern face.

Lindsey sighed. "I thought I had them straightened out, Mrs. Holdstrom."

"It's like I told you the other night, I don't blame them. I blame their folks. They let those kids run around like wild Indians."

"They do a lot of damage?"

"Ran right straight through my roses."

Lindsey shook his head. I had the sense that he was genuinely angry about the kids. It's the niggling things that get to us. In some ways a lawman can deal with a murder much more easily than he can a stupid little crime committed over and over again by the same people.

"Well, I can't go right now, Mrs. Holdstrom. But I'll handle it later tonight."

"If the mister was alive, he would've taken a shotgun to 'em. He always said that sometimes a man just had to take the law into his own hands."

Lindsey smiled at me, then looked at her. "Well, I know you're mad, Mrs. Holdstrom, and I sure don't blame you, but I don't think trampling roses is a killing offense."

"Well, he would've scared 'em off for good, at least." She turned at the door and said, "It won't do any good to just talk to them. A hickory stick is what's needed here."

She went out.

Lindsey smiled. "The little bastards. I wouldn't mind takin' a shotgun to them, myself."

Chapter 20

A small lamp burned deep in the dusk darkness as I peered in through the front window of the real estate office. A heavy man in a white shirt, the collar open and the cravat hanging free, bent over papers on a desk, a long pen in a pudgy hand made golden by the lamp glow. I knocked on the window and he looked up. He shouted something I couldn't hear, but with the wave off he gave me it was easy to guess that he'd said he was closed for the day.

I knocked again. This time he set his pen down and put on a big theatrical frown. My impression of fatness disappeared when he stood up. He was burly. And surly. A real-estate man, you think of as civilized. But I had the sense, as he stalked toward the front of the office, that he'd probably cleaned out a few saloons in his time.

He damned near ripped the door off its hinges.

"I take it you haven't learned how to read yet?" It was chilly enough now to see your breath. Two dragons talking.

"I can read any word as long as it's got under four letters in it."

"The sign says CLOSED."

"That's too long a word for me, I guess."

I wasn't making a friend here. "Who the hell are you?"

I showed him my badge.

"What the hell's an Army investigator want with me?"

"How about we go inside?"

"I have to? I mean, can I refuse?"

"You can refuse, but it wouldn't do you a hell of a lot of good."

"I've got a wife waiting dinner."

"You didn't look like you were in much of a hurry when you were working at your desk."

The frown grew even more impressive. He turned around and stalked back into the shadows.

I glanced up at the stars. They looked damned cold, damned indifferent. When they looked like that, or struck me that way, I always wanted to be inside somewhere with a glass of whiskey and a book or a magazine and a fire going, away from their alien, maybe even sinister, light.

He turned up the lamp and took his seat. Even though I hadn't been invited, I sat down.

"You rent out a hunting cabin over on Parson's Cairn." I explained the one I was talking about.

The eyes went a little funny on me. He knew that I knew something that might be some kind of trouble for him and he didn't like it at all.

"So?"

"I was out there. Went inside and looked around."

"I'm not sure that's legal."

"We can always talk to the county attorney."

"Just get the hell to the point."

"I found blood on the floor."

"Of course you found blood on the floor. Hunters use the cabin. Sometimes they bring in whatever they killed. You make it sound suspicious or something."

"I think it's human blood."

"I think you're full of shit."

"Somebody scrubbed it down as fine as they could. You don't see it unless sunlight strikes it directly."

"Funny nobody else has ever mentioned it. Till somebody like you comes along."

Every answer got increasingly belligerent. I knew he knew that I was close to something.

"Ten months ago you rented that cabin to four men who sell arms for a living."

"I'd have to check that out."

"You don't remember?"

"I rent that cabin out to a lot of different people. Why would I remember them?"

"David Ford probably set it up for them. They were visiting his ranch. You knew David Ford?"

"Yes, and I know he was your brother. So what if he set it up? So what if they stayed there a few nights?"

"A woman died. A Cree woman named Louise."

This time it was the mouth that went funny. The lips kind of crawled around over themselves, as if not quite sure which way to settle. Then he blinked violently and I realized that the lips and the blink were part of the same process, a nervous reaction.

"Yes. Louise did die. She fell and cracked her skull and drowned." He had composed himself again. "Are you supposed to be some kind of brilliant detective, Ford? The four men stayed out there and the woman cracked her skull and drowned. So what?

Separate incidents. Things like that happen all the time."

"I don't think that's how it happened."

"Well, when you can prove it happened otherwise, come back and talk to me. Right now I intend to go home and have dinner with my wife."

He walked over to his coatrack in the corner and picked off his derby. "You want to talk any more, Mr. Ford, you'll have to arrest me. Barring that, I want you to get the hell out of my office so that I can leave."

This time he walked to the front door, turning down the lamp as he passed it. His footsteps were loud in the sudden gloom. The shadows became sinister. He knew a secret—a secret I was beginning to understand—and his deceit lent everything an unclean quality. A nice comfortable little life that he didn't want to disturb, even though a woman had been murdered. The secret was in the air of the place.

He locked up without saying a word. He walked quickly away when he was finished, leaving me to stand alone in the night. Saloon music, the fainter sound of a few wagons and buggies headed home, the lonesome bark of dogs in the night.

The lobby of Brinkley's hotel was busy with guests who'd just come in on a train. Two women in dusty silk dresses and their husbands in dusty dark business suits. They were piling bags up on the frail old arms of a colored man and taking pains to make him understand their contempt for him. His arms were filled with four large bags piled on top of each other and they weren't done yet.

"For God's sake, if you can't even hold a few bags, they should get somebody else."

"Hold still, will you? I'm trying to put another bag on top here."

"Don't expect any kind of remuneration. I heard that word you just called my husband under your breath."

They were lovely people; they ran the world, just ask them. There seem to be more and more of them these days, everywhere you go. Sleek and rich and arrogant.

Since I was going up the stairs anyway, I grabbed the two bags they were determined to pile on top of the already four-deep pile.

"And just who might you be?" said the woman as I took her bag. The eyes sparked disapproval of my range clothes.

"His boss. I help out with the overflow."

"But you're wearing a gun," said her husband.

I winked at the colored man. "This is a dangerous hotel."

"Well, maybe we shouldn't stay here, Theodore," said the woman.

"This isn't a dangerous hotel," Theodore said. "I looked it up in the brochure and the brochure said that it was perfectly nice and perfectly safe."

"Perfectly," said his friend. "I read the same brochure Theodore did."

The colored man went up ahead of me. He swayed a lot. I thought he might fall over. But he made it up the steep stairs.

He set the bags down and got the door opened. "I thank you, mister."

"I was coming up here, anyway. See a man named Brinkley."

"Oh, yeah, Brinkley. I don't think he come back from supper yet."

You could hear them coming up the stairs. The women with their birdy chatter, the men with their gruff, somber voices discussing how things should go in this world of ours.

The old man was listening to them, too.

"How can you stand 'em?" I said.

He grinned out of his ancient black face. "Barely is how I can stand 'em, mister. Barely."

I left before I'd have to see them again.

Brinkley wasn't in, or at least he wasn't answering my knock. I went down the back stairs. I didn't want to see four world rulers again.

I walked back to my hotel. The clerk said there were no messages. I went up to my room.

Brinkley was waiting for me. Somebody had tied him to a straight-back chair, blindfolded and gagged him, and then rammed a long kitchen knife deep into his heart.

I locked my door from the inside and got to work.

I went through his pockets. There wasn't much use to doing it, of course. The killer would have done it thoroughly. Anything left behind would be worthless.

Death has a way of becoming routine. That's the secret of war. If it didn't become routine, you'd have most of your troops shooting their leaders and heading back home. It's a matter of accretion. First you see one body and then you see a couple of bodies and in no time at all you're ready to see your first *pile* of bodies. Then you're just what your commander wants you to be. A man who sees death as routine.

I had just turned away from Brinkley, toward the door and the stairs and the street that would take me over to Marshal Wickham's office where I'd tell him about yet another corpse, when whoever it was made a terrible mistake by making a single but noisy move in the closet.

Instinct took over. Out came my gun. Up went my heart rate. Narrow became the width of my eyes as they focused on the closet door.

The heroic thing to do would have been to storm the door and fling it open. And someday it'd be nice to be reckless and heroic like that. Say on the day when the doc told me that with my newly diagnosed disease he'd give me about thirty-six hours to live. That would be the time to be reckless and heroic, when it wouldn't matter anymore. When it would be better to just get it over with, anyway. But right now I looked forward to several more years of breathing, so I stood where I was and said, "C'mon out before I start shooting. I pump enough bullets into that closet door, I'm bound to kill you."

"Don't shoot. Please."

The voice was familiar, but as yet I couldn't put a name to it.

"I'll come out with my hands up."

"Good. Then do it."

The door was flung open and out stumbled Wayland. He had his hands up way over his head and he was biting his lower lip. He said, "Brinkley there. I didn't kill him. I came up here to talk to you and I heard a groaning—he was all bound up like this. But he wasn't dead. Not quite. And then I heard you coming and jumped in the closet."

"You didn't hear anybody else?"

"No."

"Why'd you come up to talk to me?"

He looked at Brinkley. "It was time somebody told you the truth."

"Yeah? And that's what you were going to do?"

"I couldn't handle it anymore."

"Handle what?"

"Waiting to die. Till it was my turn to be killed."

The old belligerence was gone. He was broken now. A boy, no longer a man. I pointed the barrel of my gun exactly at his stomach and said, "You have a gun?"

"A shoulder setup."

"Throw the gun on the bed. But first take off your coat so I can see you handle the gun. No surprises or I'll kill you on the spot."

"That's all there is on this trip." He said it with a sob in his voice. "Killing and killing and killing. I want out of this place and this life. I don't give a damn if my father approves of me or not. I'm going to be a schoolteacher. He doesn't think that's 'manly' enough for the family name. But to hell with him."

"The gun."

"Oh. Yes. Sorry."

He carefully took off his suit coat and flung it on the bed. He had a small, expensive shoulder rig and a small, expensive .32 riding in it.

"Now the gun."

He took it out with the tips of his fingers.

"Maybe if I throw it on the bed, it'll go off." He really was scared.

"Then walk it over there and put it down nice and gentle."

"You probably think I'm a sissy, the way I act. My old man thinks I'm a sissy. He's always told people that. Even when I was standing right next to him."

"Look, I'm sorry about you and your old man. But mostly I don't give a shit. Right now I'm going to take you down to the bar and buy you a drink and you're going to tell me what's going on. I've got an idea, but I need to hear it confirmed."

He seemed surprised. He nodded to Brinkley. "You're just going to leave him here?"

"You think he's going to get up and walk away? We'll lock the door. Nobody should bother him. There were four of you. Now you're the only one left."

"I know," he said, wistfully. "I didn't like them. They were a lot like my old man. But I didn't hate them enough to want to see them get killed like that."

"You can put your arms down now."

He glanced at one of his arms. It seemed to look strange to him, as if he'd never seen an arm before, and was trying to figure out exactly what it was and exactly what it did.

"Oh, yeah. Thanks. They were kind've getting numb. Up in the air like that, I mean."

I checked the room one more time, trying to make sure that I hadn't overlooked anything. I didn't find anything.

"He's starting to smell," Wayland said. He didn't

sound disgusted or put off especially. He just remarked on it, as if he'd never been around anybody who'd been killed recently. As maybe he hadn't.

"Yeah," I said. "He does sort of stink. Now let's go get you that drink."

Chapter 21

As I'd told Wayland, I had a pretty good idea of what had happened to Louise that night on Parson's Cairn.

The four men in the cabin—three of them dead now—wouldn't have known who she was. And they would've been too drunk to care, anyway. Four drunks and a woman and a night of need and lust.

Wayland said that it had started out as nothing more than a polite invitation. Louise had been looking for a stray kitten hiding somewhere on the island. She'd passed the cabin. Wayland and the others spotted her. Invited her in. She knew about men, especially drunken men, so she refused. But she relented when she agreed to sit on the porch with them and have a beer. She was kind of tired from her two-hour search. She wasn't a drinker, but maybe half a glass would be all right. They made everything even better by saying they'd go looking for the kitten, too, soon as they had a few more drinks.

They had quite a few more drinks. She tried to get away, but every time she made a move to do so one of the men grabbed her and dragged her back. Wayland, sensing what was coming, tried to help her escape at one point. He got a black eye and some busted teeth for his trouble.

Wayland didn't see the actual rape, but he heard it. They threw him out of the cabin. He didn't have a gun. There was no way to overpower them. He thought of taking the boat and going for help. But by the time he found anybody, they would be done with her.

All he could do was listen to her scream, cry out to Wayland for help. He'd never felt less manly, more impotent. He'd even covered his ears so he didn't have to listen to her. Through it all the three men were laughing. They didn't seem to understand that they were raping a woman. They were just having themselves a good time. Several times Spenser bellered that they were going to make this worth her while. Money, of course. Money healed all wounds, right? Didn't everybody know that?

Then it was done. For a time the laughter continued, but it was diminished somehow and continued to recede in enthusiasm. They were slowly beginning to understand, as they started to sober up, what they'd done. Then he heard them, one by one, making their apologies to her, asking her what she'd like them to buy her. And then she told them who her friend was. The very same marshal who'd greeted them on their arrival in town the other day. Charley Wickham.

Wayland said that he would like to have seen their faces when she told them. They were already regretting what they'd done. But now their faces, old and harsh in the hangover light of the kerosene lamps, would reflect fear. Terror. This was serious business now. They hadn't raped just anybody. If she was telling the truth, and they all knew she was, they'd raped the marshal's woman.

Wayland wasn't sure who'd first suggested the idea. But, standing outside the door, Wayland knew he'd have to do something and do it quickly.

The door opened. They had a gag across her mouth, her arms tied behind her.

Wayland had armed himself with a good chunk of two-by-four he'd found in a pile around back. His first victim was Brinkley. He hit him so hard across the back of the head that he thought he'd killed him. Then the other two men were on him. He swung the two-by-four at them several times but they weren't about to be stopped. Too much at stake. They had to get rid of both Wayland and Louise now.

Louise used the turmoil to escape. She ran through the woods, presumably toward her own cabin. From here, Wayland and the others could only speculate on what happened. The island had a single steep cliff. There was a narrow, foot-worn trail along it that Louise used frequently. As she did that night. But that night, with all the terror, she lost her footing and slipped. Nobody had ever survived a fall from that particular cliff. The record remained unbroken. She didn't survive, either. They spent the rest of the night dragging her body back up to shore.

Brinkley, recovering from Wayland's assault, persuaded the others to let Wayland live. His death would be too difficult to explain. And Wayland couldn't tell the marshal what happened because all three of them would tell the marshal that Wayland was a part of it. However many grim years they would serve in prison, Wayland would serve, too.

They went back to town, paid their visit to David in the morning right on schedule, and then waited to be visited by the marshal. It would be a routine inquiry, but a sensible one. They'd been on the island when she'd slipped and fell. Perhaps they knew something. No, they'd say, but they understood that the marshal was only doing his job and they'd help any way they could.

Then a queer thing happened—or didn't happen. The body was found, all right, but the man who ran the mortuary and was also the county medical examiner pronounced Louise Skelly's death an accident. No suggestion of foul play, he'd said. The presiding judge then saw fit to close the case.

The men spent another three days in town, each trying to bribe David into giving them first bid on the amazing weapon he'd created. But David wasn't finished working on the gun and wouldn't sell it. Say what you would about David—he might be a ladies' man and an imbiber and a brawler—but he took pride in his work. On the day they were to leave, they each received their first blackmail letter from James. He knew what had happened to Louise and who had killed her.

"We went our separate ways," Wayland said. "But it didn't matter. The blackmail letters kept coming. And we kept sending him money. Then your brother let us know that he'd about brought the gun up to speed so we had to come back here, which none of us were happy about."

"And then somebody started killing you off."

"Exactly." He sighed, sat staring at the table.

"One thing," I said.

He didn't look up. "What?"

"You'll need to testify to all this."

When he did look up, his face was that of a sad child's. "Wait till my old man hears about this one. He'll just say that I fucked up all over again. And he'll be right." He made a face. "Will I go to prison for withholding evidence?"

"Depends on the judge. But if you get anybody short of a hanging judge, you'll probably get the charges dropped for your cooperation."

"You know what's really funny?"

"What?"

"All this dying—and nobody knows where the gun is."

"I've got an idea where it might be," I said.

"Where?"

"That one I need to keep to myself."

I picked up my hat. "I've got business to tend to. They've got a couple attorneys in town here. Figure out which you think is the best one and pay him a visit."

He sighed. "I don't have much money. I'll probably have to ask the old man. God, I can hear the sermons he'll give me. He'll ride my ass till the day he dies."

As I was standing up, I said, "I'm sorry, Wayland. But right now your old man isn't worth arguing about. You need to get yourself a lawyer and then you need to go see the county attorney here and get this whole thing in process."

"You put in a good word for me, Ford?"

"Sure. I'm not sure how much good it'll do. A lot of these people resent Federales, as they call them. But I'll be glad to speak up to anybody who'll listen."

He laughed bitterly. "I'm getting a good look at our so-called justice system. It doesn't work worth a damn. Everybody brings all their prejudices to it and it just breaks down."

"Not all the time."

"Most of the time."

I laughed myself. "Well, some of the time."

Two older women were soaking lace handkerchiefs with their tears. Black silk dresses with bustles so big leprechauns could sit on them. Their sobs echoed off the walls of the small visitation room in the mortuary vestibule. The air smelled of flowers and death. One of the women glared at me as if I'd personally killed the person she was mourning.

I went down the short hall to the business office. The door was open an inch. I opened it wider and went inside.

Beth Cave wasn't typing today. She stood in her black dress at a wooden filing cabinet, inserting one file folder into a long line of others. Her back was to me. The sobs of the women in the vestibule had covered any sounds I made. When she turned around, she looked shocked to find me there, as if I'd appeared by some kind of evil magic.

"He's not in."

"I didn't want to see him, anyway."

"I'm not in either," she said, walking primly to her desk. For the first time I realized that in her younger days she might well have been attractive. But work or life or maybe both together had soured and blanched her in a now permanent way. She sat down and said, "You'll just waste your time here. I have absolutely nothing to say to you."

I said, "I talked to the county attorney."

"Mr. Philbrick."

"Yes," I lied. "Mr. Philbrick."

"We just buried his aunt here a few months ago."

In another circumstance, I probably would have smiled. You work at a livery, you think of people in terms of their horses and vehicles. You work at a barbershop, you think of people in terms of their hair. You work at a mortuary, you think of people in terms of their kin you helped bury.

I started to speak, but then one of the weeping women poked her head in the door. She had plump cheeks raw from crying and a pair of store-bought teeth that gleamed in a way no real teeth ever had. I wanted to feel properly sorry for her but I couldn't quite. I guess it was the way she still glared at me. I was in range clothes again. Her husband probably hired and fired men like me all the time. "We want the best carriage, Miss Cave."

"Of course. I'll see to it personally."

"And we don't want Mary Beth Guterman in the choir. My brother always thought she sang off-key. He even said that to the parson many times. You'd think for all the money my brother gave that church the parson would at least have taken Mary Beth Guterman out of the choir."

"No Mary Beth Guterman. You can be assured of that."

"We have people coming all the way from St. Louis. Very wealthy people. They're used to the best. We want to show them that we appreciate the best, too. We don't just throw our loved ones in the ground like barbarians."

"Of course not, Mrs. Winters. We'll give him the

same kind of funeral he'd get at the very best parlor in St. Louis."

"Or Chicago."

"Or Chicago, yes, for that matter. You know we buy a lot of supplies from Chicago."

"You do? Well, you should advertise that. Right in that announcement you make in the paper each week. People like to know things like that. All the way from Chicago."

Just then the other woman in the vestibule doubled the volume of her grief.

"My poor sister-in-law," Mrs. Winters clucked. "This has been so difficult on her. Especially with all the gossip about how my brother ran around on her, which is of course ridiculous."

"Of course it is," Beth Cave soothed.

Another blast of sobbing from the vestibule.

"Well, I'd best tend to her."

Another glare aimed at me and she was gone.

"You should follow her right out that door, Mr. Ford."

"Do you enjoy your life, Miss Cave?"

"And just what's that supposed to mean?"

"I mean you seem to enjoy what you have. I'm sure you have some good friends and some things you enjoy doing with them. And your place is probably fixed up nice. And you're a member in good standing in your church . . ."

"Just what is the point of this?"

"That it could all come to an end. That the county attorney will be coming after your boss very soon now. And that if I ask him to, he could charge you for withholding evidence. And if he won't, I'll find a federal judge who will."

"That's ridiculous. I haven't done anything."

"The other day you started to tell me about the night they brought Louise in here. You must've been working late. You saw what she looked like. And you realized that your boss filed a false death certificate. He forgot to add that she was beaten and raped, didn't he? He made it sound like a simple little accident, a woman losing her footing in the rain along the cliff and . . ."

Her glance warned me, but too late. Way too late. The sobbing of the women had covered his footsteps. All I had time to do was start to turn and duck but Newcomb was too fast for me.

He clipped me hard across the back side of my head, and as I started to pitch forward he got me a second time, with much more force, across the top of my head. The last thing I heard was the women in the vestibule crying.

Darkness. The smell of newly sawn wood. Pine. Then the sharp stink of chemicals I recognized as belonging to Newcomb's profession of mortician. I tried to extend my arms from my sides. I could push them outward less than an inch.

Like most people of these times, I had the fear of being buried alive. A lot of that had gone on in Europe after the last sweep of plague a couple decades back. To a much lesser degree, it had also gone on over here. A couple of enterprising businessmen had cashed in on the fear. There were coffins that had bells you could ring in case you were buried inside. There were caskets with breathing tubes that came up out of the ground. There were caskets that were sunk with less than a foot of dirt atop them and lids that could be easily pushed upward if need be. For people who didn't want to spend any money, family groups were known to have burial watches. Family members took turns sitting on a chair next to the burial site for as long as three or four days following the ceremony, just to make sure old Uncle Bob didn't start screaming to let him out.

I was in a coffin. There had been enough air to keep me alive for a while, but that while was slipping away fast. Unfortunately, the lid wasn't the break-away kind. Newcomb's shoddy craftsmanship hadn't extended to the nails. They had firmly fixed the lid in place. There wasn't even a bell for me to ring.

I became conscious of every breath I took. Images of being buried alive always included being planted several feet down in the earth. There was a good chance I was going to suffocate sitting in some mortician's back room.

Distant conversations. A door opening and closing somewhere far away. Out back, workmen pulling a clattering buckboard up to the door. A contralto voice—a church singer rehearsing, probably up in the visitation room. Just another ordinary day in the death business, except for the Army investigator suffocating in a newly made coffin in the backroom.

I started working on the lid. Not being a masterpiece of construction, this pine box shouldn't be too hard to escape. I started slowly, quietly pushing upward on the lid with my one good arm. I spent several minutes before I realized that, shoddy as this box was, the lid wasn't going to give. The air started to get tainted with my own sour breath.

The coffin was a rectangle. I pressed the soles of my boots against the front of the box. I could apply more pressure with my feet than I could with my hand. I went to work. After the first five minutes or so I started thinking that maybe this wouldn't work any better than the lid would.

Yes, I could kick out the front of the coffin easily enough. But to do it I'd have to make too much noise. By the time I'd freed myself from the rest of the box, Newcomb would've heard me and come back here with a gun.

My breathing was starting to thin, get shallower with each breath. No dizziness yet, but I couldn't hold out forever. I tried to remember the setup in Newcomb's backroom. There were empty coffins stacked against one wall. There was the large table where he worked on the corpses. And then there were the two saw-horses next to the worktable. He'd had an empty coffin sitting there, presumably so he and his workmen could put the body in it when Newcomb was finished with his work. I wondered about trying to force my coffin off the sawhorses and then realized that I was beginning to panic. Think of what a hell of a noise the coffin hitting the floor would make.

I pushed with my arm and legs again, trying to find any vulnerable spot in the coffin. My best chance was still the front end, kicking out with my feet.

I hadn't experienced the sensation of suffocating yet. But it was starting to work on me. The coffin seemed much smaller than it had a few minutes ago. And darker. And now it was silent. No conversations in the dim distance up front. No wagon chink or horse neigh in the alley. No sobbing anywhere.

The coffin was beginning to shrink even tighter. I knew that soon enough I would start smashing my way out of here. Panic. Survival. Anything but giving in to the slow siphoning of breathable air. I would be alive, yes, but for how long? I'd be back in Newcomb's gunsights again. He'd make it easy on himself. He'd kill me quick.

I was starting to press upward with my hand when I heard what sounded like footsteps. Quick, soft footsteps. Newcomb would make more noise than that.

Then Newcomb's voice in the dim distance up front: "Where're you going, Beth? I need to dictate that letter."

"I just need to get some more paper from the storage room, Mr. Newcomb."

"Well, hurry up, will you? I want to get this letter dictated. Then I have to get over to Rotary for a meeting."

"Well, you certainly wouldn't want to miss Rotary."

The quiet footsteps kept moving toward me during the conversation. I wondered if Beth Cave knew I was back here in the coffin. Even if she did, it was doubtful she'd help me. She was comfortable in her life here and part of that comfort was a good job. She'd made it obvious that she didn't want to risk losing that job.

Then she was at the coffin. Whispering. "If you can hear me, knock once with your knuckle."

I didn't even think about what this might mean. It could be some kind of ruse, a way to find out if I was alive without going through the task of taking the nails out of the coffin.

I knocked lightly with my knuckle against the coffin lid.

"I'm going to help you," she whispered.

A minute went by. Footsteps. The faint clanking of tools being moved around. Apparently she was looking for something.

"Are you about ready, Beth?" Newcomb shouted from the front of the place.

"I'll be right there, Mr. Newcomb."

"I don't have all day."

"I know, Mr. Newcomb. Rotary."

At any other time, in any other circumstance, I would have smiled at the way she was able to put so much malice in the word "Rotary." All her contempt for her boss was in the scorn she was able to pack into that word. Newcomb wasn't the subtle type, apparently. He didn't seem to hear what she was really doing with the word.

The coffin shrank a few more inches. I had no idea why, but my rigid, anxious body was now slick with sweat. Cold sweat.

"I'm on my way, Mr. Newcomb," she called.

And beneath the sound of her voice was another sound. At first I didn't know what it was. But then it came clear.

The metal claws of a crowbar gently opening the lid of the coffin. Not all the way up. Just enough to let in air. Just enough to let me do the rest myself.

She whispered, "That's the best I can do, Mr. Ford."

She was gone by the time I could whisper a thank you in return. I lay there, cooler air sluicing in through the half inch she'd raised a small part of the coffin lid.

Her footsteps told me that she went hurriedly down the hall, stopped, opened a door of some kind, took something out—the paper she needed, apparently—and then continued her way back to Newcomb's office.

"I was beginning to wonder if you'd snuck off on me," Newcomb said.

"Oh, yes, that's something I do often, isn't it, Mr. Newcomb? Sneak off on you."

"Now, now, none of your smart mouth. It's what I've told you before, Beth. I think that's the biggest reason you've never been able to find a husband. Men don't like women with smart mouths."

"I was wondering what my trouble was, Mr. Newcomb, and I guess you've figured it out for me."

Mr. Newcomb didn't complain about that particular smart-mouth remark. Either it was too subtle for him or he was just tired of the banter. "Are you ready now? Can we finally get this letter dictated?"

"Anytime you're ready," she said. She was back to being prim and dutiful.

I started work on the coffin. She'd made it easy. I worked slowly, a few inches at a time. I still couldn't afford to have Newcomb hear me.

The coffin, as I'd suspected, was lying across two sawhorses. The next thing would be climbing down without making any noise. Rather than go to the floor, I stepped out of the coffin onto the blood-stained table where Newcomb practiced his dark craft. I walked across the table, stepped down onto a chair, and from the chair stepped to the floor.

Newcomb had done me the favor of covering my escape with his shouting. He was dictating a surly letter to a maker of headstones, telling them how shoddy their work had become in the last several months, and how customer complaints had become a daily battle for him.

But I didn't feel much sympathy. I had a battle of my own to fight. I went looking for everybody's favorite marshal, one Charley Wickham.

Chapter 22

I spent an hour looking for him. Office, livery, saloons, even his home. Nobody had seen him.

As I walked past the depot, I saw several long, wooden crates being loaded onto a cart that would be brought up to the next train to pull in. The two men doing the loading didn't look particularly impressed with me when I approached them. I probably looked pretty rough after my time in the coffin. The coffin hadn't done much for my wound, either. The cramped quarters had made the lancing pain sharp and frequent again.

With my good hand, I reached in and dug out my identification. I showed it to the bald one. Even though the day was turning into long shadows and chilly breezes, he wiped the back of his forehead off with the back of his hand and said, "Pete, better look at this."

Pete said, "He don't read too good and neither do I." He squinted at it.

"The print says I'm a Federal agent working for the United States Army. That badge says pretty much the same thing."

"Pretty fancy badge."

"They give me that instead of a lot of money."

My joke loosened Pete up. "All right. What can we do for you?"

"This all you got to load for the next train?"

The bald man spoke. "There's another cartload back there."

"I'd like to look through the freight."

"Anything special you looking for?"

I couldn't tell him. He might be kin to Wickham. Or he might want to have Wickham owe him a favor. "Afraid I can't go into that."

The bald man said, "Let me have a look at that badge again." I handed him the identification Pete had just handed back to me.

The bald man studied the bright badge a moment and said, "Well, I guess you are who you say you are. We was gonna go grab a little coffee, anyways. We got another two hours before the train gets in and we don't have much else to do but wait around."

"Might as well help yourself," Pete said.

With the onset of dusk and lamplight filling the depot windows, there was that sense of loneliness that always comes with the dying day. The exterior of the depot was as empty as the long, gleaming, silver tracks themselves.

I didn't find anything much on the cart near the depot platform. Most of the crates seemed to be some kind of farm tools being shipped from a small factory here to points farther west of here. Nothing suspicious, nothing even very interesting.

I had much better luck on the cart near the back of the depot. Six crates of various sizes. There was just enough light to read the one that was being sent to a

Mrs. Marie Wickham in Normal, Missouri. Seems like the marshal was sending his mom a gift.

This was the one I was looking for. It was on the bottom of a stack of four other crates. Meaning that there was no way I could get to it with just one useful arm and hand. I walked to the other side of the depot, looking for Pete and his friend. They'd said they were going to take a break. Most breaks consisted of sitting down somewhere on the premises and rolling yourself a smoke to go along with your cup of coffee.

But I couldn't find Pete and his friend anywhere. I started looking for the depot manager, but was told by the gent in the ticket window that the manager had gone home early with a bad cold. "Should a heard him cough," the ticket man said, "sonofabitch sounded like he was dyin', is what it sounded like. I had a cousin, shirttail cousin I guess you'd say, sounded like that and two days later he was dead. You shouldn't take no chances when your cough gets like that. No, sir. Shouldn't take no chances at all."

I went to the platform. Dusk was sucking up all the daylight. You could see the lonesome lines of railroad track below the cold, distant stars. The wind came all the way down from the mountains. It smelled and tasted of snow. But it was clean and fresh and for a moment took away the pain in my wound.

I walked to the edge of the platform and moved down the three steps to the ground. I saw Pete and his friend walking toward me. They were coming from a long ways away, a lot longer than you'd expect them to be on a break. They'd brought another friend along. In the shadows of early evening he sure looked an awful lot like Marshal Wickham.

Wickham knew what he was doing. He would already have had a deputy or two come on ahead and move in on me. The next minute or two, they'd show themselves and arrest me. Any direction I headed, they'd have me trapped.

I went back inside the depot. The ticket window was part of a small office. I knocked on the door. The window man shuffled over, opened it, and said, "Oh, it's you."

His eyes dropped down and saw the Colt I was holding on him.

I told him who I was and what I wanted. He wanted identification. I moved my gun to the hand jutting from the sling and dug out my badge. He looked it over. Handed it back, all right.

"There going to be shootin'?"

"Hope not. Now move aside."

"I sure don't want to get shot. And you sure don't look like good luck." He nodded to my sling.

No more time for talk. I pushed past him. Closed the door behind me. Moved to the back of the one-desk, two-file-cabinet office and crouched down in the shadows.

I heard the front door swing open and heard Wickham say, "Bill, we're looking for a man named Noah Ford. He's pretending to be a Federal agent. But actually he's the man done all the killing lately."

"Nobody been in here for the last twenty minutes," Bill said.

The problem was that I couldn't see his face. He

stood at his ticket window. With his back to me I couldn't see what his expression was. It would be easy enough for him to signal Wickham.

"Maybe you missed him," Wickham said. "Maybe there was a crowd. Tall, lean fella. Hard-lookin' face. Arm in a sling."

"Think I'd remember the sling, Marshal. Afraid I just didn't see him."

"Well, we're gonna look in the storage room in the back."

The sweat came back. Cold sweat, hospital sweat, wound sweat. I'd pushed too hard since leaving the hospital. Now I was stuck back here behind the desk, hungry, cold, damning myself for setting myself up in a trap like this. Any way you cut it, Wickham was going to grab me sooner or later. I had to resist the impulse to just stand up and start shooting.

"Well, thanks, Bill," Wickham said. But the way he said it revealed a lot more than he imagined. Because his voice had a wink in it. The secret had been passed between the two. Wickham knew I was back here and now he was going to act on it.

Well, not act on it personally. For that he had a deputy I'd never seen before open the office door and without any hesitation at all, start emptying one of two six-guns at the desk I was hiding behind. The noise, the smoke, the ticket clerk shouting and cussing and praying, and all about the same time, only added to the confusion I felt. Confusion that was clarified when, just as the last bullet was fired, I heard heavy footsteps enter the office and Wickham say, "I've got a shotgun here, Ford. Whether I use it or not is up to you. You've got a bad arm and I reckon you've overworked yourself since leaving the hospital. Now put your gun down and we'll talk this thing over."

I thought of a couple things I could say, but they would just be foolish things said by a foolish man fast running out of luck and strength.

"Save yourself some bullets, Marshal."

"You know better than to try anything."

"I'm going to slide my gun across the floor and then get up and put my hands in the air. How's that?"

"Get moving."

I hadn't mentioned my Bowie knife. But then that wasn't any of his business. That had been a gift from my brother David. And it was between me and him.

I did what I promised to do and I did it slow and easy and obvious, the way you do it when you want to avoid having a lawman put a whole lot of lead in your chest. He had an unerring eye, Wickham did. He watched my every move carefully.

When I slid my Colt over to him he didn't even stoop to pick it up. He wanted his eyes on me. He just kicked the Colt off to the side.

"Now the hands. Up in the air."

"You charging me with anything in particular?"

"The hands, Ford. In the air."

I put them in the air. "I have a citizen's right to know what I'm being charged with."

"Now what do you think, Ford? You're a smart Federale. You know what you did. I don't need to tell you that."

"I'm not sure, but I can guess."

"Be my guest."

"You're going to charge me with the murder of my brother and the three arms merchants."

"You forgot a couple of people, but keep going."

"You think maybe I assassinated old Abe Lincoln and pinned it on Booth?"

"Walk toward me. Slow. And keep the hands in the air."

The next five minutes were routine. He got me in handcuffs, he repeated the charges for his deputies to hear. I tried to figure out how he was going to kill me between here and the jail. I wasn't going to help him. I wasn't going to make any kind of move that could be misinterpreted as trying to make a break. I was going to do what he told me to do and make it obvious.

But he'd figure out a way to kill me. He had to. I knew everything now. I was the only thing standing between him and his old hometown where the gun was being shipped. He could relax there for a while and when the federal hunt for the gun wasn't so hot, he could quietly sell it on the black market and have all the money he'd need for the rest of his life. And me? Washington had warned me not to get involved in my own brother's case. But I knew better. I was going to give him a chance to escape—after I had secured the weapon. But things hadn't worked out quite that way. And it would be no trouble for Wickham to make a convincing enough case to Washington that I'd been so upset about the murder of my brother—said murderer still conveniently on the loose—that I just started killing people in a crazed attempt to find his murderer. So Wickham, good and true lawman that he was, was forced to track me down and shoot me. Washington wouldn't be surprised. Hell, they might even give Wickham one of those citations they're always so eager to hand out.

Then he said it and it all came clear. "He knows where his brother's gun is," he said to his deputy. "And he's going to take me there and we're going to get this whole thing all wrapped up."

No sense in murdering me in cold blood in front of witnesses when a nice little buggy ride could take us out somewhere in the country where the only witnesses would be birds and frogs. And they were both notoriously unreliable in a courtroom.

So he had his ruse going well—pretending to still be searching for the gun while in fact it was in a crate not far away, about to be shipped to his old ancestral home—and he had me in tow, about to rid himself of the last person blocking him from his getaway and his money.

He did it right. And he did just what I thought he'd do.

We walked over to the livery where the men I'd gotten to know all kept staring at my handcuffs. Marshal Wickham ordered up a buggy and a horse, and while that was being readied for him, he explained to his audience what he'd explained to his men—that I was the killer everybody was so nervous about and that I was going to show him where this weapon was that so many had died for.

Then we were on the dusty road—a rifle on one side of him, his Colt in his holster on my side, plenty of firepower to kill me with—the new buggy nice and easy on the relatively smooth patch of road. Over the thrum and whir of the wheels, I said, "You see their faces?"

"Whose faces you talking about?"

"The men at the livery. Or your own men, for that matter."

"What about their faces?"

I didn't say anything for a time. I let my question work on him, as I knew it would. My friends the night folks were out now—the owls and stray dogs and raccoons and so many, many others that pass through the shadows unnoticed. The wind was up and it was cold, but oddly enough the chill only added to the hard imperious beauty of the full golden moon. Even the starlight seemed more vivid tonight.

"I asked you, what about their faces?"

He was getting nervous. It hadn't been just my question. Everything that had happened these past few days, everything that he'd done, was starting to overwhelm him. It had to. It had been too much.

"Your story about me. They didn't believe it."

"Oh, they believed it all right. Because I said it. I've never lied to them."

"Until now."

He glanced at me. "All right. Until now. And what I did was justifiable and you'd better damned well believe that. You know what happened, Ford. You've figured it all out. They killed Louise. They raped her and then they killed her. But they wouldn't have had to pay for it. They haul some fancy-ass Eastern lawyer back here and they'd get reduced sentences. A few years. Nothing."

He looked straight ahead again. "When my wife died, Louise took my life over. She got me through it. I never had a friend like her. And then one day I fell in love with her. She was the most decent woman I've ever known. And they raped her. One right after the other. I try not to think about it, what it must have been like for somebody like her."

"But why kill my brother?"

"Because he brought them here. He also knew what they'd done and he didn't step forward to say anything. He didn't give a damn about Louise. He just wanted money for his gun."

"You didn't need to cut his throat."

"He would've screamed otherwise. And I'd spotted you sneaking up to the barn. A gunshot would've made too much noise."

"He was my brother."

"I thought you hated him. That was my impression."

"Whatever I felt for him, he was still my brother. Kin. Blood. However you want to say it."

I did it then. Even handcuffed, it wasn't all that difficult. He had way too much faith in the ability of his handcuffs to inhibit my actions. He was also too caught up in his memories of Louise to take note of how I waited until we hit a rough patch, which jolted the entire small buggy off one of its wheels and jounced us together on the narrow seat of the narrow buggy.

I reached down and jerked his Colt from its holster. I didn't do it with any grace. I couldn't. For one thing, the road was still bouncing the buggy around. For another, graceful hand movement is impossible when you're wearing a pair of steel handcuffs.

He knew instantly what I was doing. But it was already too late. He grabbed and slapped for my hand. But my hand was already gone.

He lurched for me. I leaned as far away as the confines of the buggy would allow. It wasn't hard to hold on to the Colt. It wasn't hard to put my finger on the trigger, either. "I'm going to kill you, Wickham. If you want it now, just tell me."

His body made a lot of small, old-man noises, the stomach and the throat and the nose, gurgle, wheeze, sniff. He was packing a whole lot of years on him and they were starting to fail him now. He didn't have all that long even if I let him go, a few years here or there. What he had to decide—because he knew damned well I wasn't bluffing—was whether or not he wanted to die right here and right now.

The shoulders slumped in silent resignation. "Shit," he said. Maybe it wasn't eloquent but there wasn't much else to say.

He leaned back and separated the reins he'd bunched in one hand. He looked straight ahead. "They killed her, Ford. I loved her."

"That's kind of funny."

"What is?"

"I didn't figure you for the type that would ask for mercy."

"You could let me go."

"You're wrong. I couldn't. That isn't in me."

He turned his face to mine. "Your brother?"

"Not just him. The others, too. A little girl nearly got killed."

"That wasn't me. That was Frank."

"You were working together. He wouldn't have been in that situation if you hadn't brought him in on the gun. He killed Gwen for no reason." Then: "Stop here."

We went a ways. There was a coyote in the dark, cold foothills and he was one sorrowful-sounding sonofabitch.

He finally pulled over. One of the horses took one of those craps that probably lightened him by ten pounds.

"I'm getting down first," I said. "You try and pull away I'll kill you right here and now."

"You didn't even like your brother."

"We've already talked about that and it won't do you any good to talk about it again."

"I loved her, can't you understand that? Can't you understand what that did to me when they killed her?"

"Maybe I could've understood it if you hadn't grabbed the gun. The gun didn't have anything to do with her."

"I wanted a few good years. I've been a reasonably honest lawman, Ford. Don't I deserve a few years at the end of the line?"

"I'm getting down now. You remember what I said about trying anything."

It was easy to see that he wanted to lash the horses and pull away. There was a chance he might even make it. There was no guarantee that if he pulled away at just the right moment I'd be able to hit him. Or hit him clean anyway. Maybe he'd get wounded slightly. A man in handcuffs. A man with one arm in a sling. He had a chance, anyway, and maybe a good one.

Another reason he might take the chance and pull away was that he was probably considering what I was considering. Justice would be him dying the same way David had. I had a Bowie knife and I'd cut a few throats before, myself, when necessary. And he sure wouldn't want to take a chance on that.

Getting down wasn't easy. Between the sling and the cuffs, I damned near slipped twice. I came so close once that he raised the reins for a second, but I caught myself, getting a better purchase on the buggy step. I raised the gun. He put the reins back down.

When I was steady on the ground, I said, "Now come around here with that key of yours and get these cuffs off me."

"Yeah?" he said, all his features lost in the deep shadow of the buggy. "Then what?"

"We'll see."

"What if I won't do it?"

"Then I'll kill you right now and drag your ass out of the buggy and go through your pockets till I find the key."

"I could take the key and throw it out in the brush somewhere."

"You want to see if you can move faster than my bullet?"

"You fucking sonofabitch."

"C'mon, Wickham. Get your ass over here."

I didn't give him the break he'd maybe expected. As he started to get down, I moved through the moonlight on the deserted sandy road. By the time he reached the ground, I was standing right there. I hadn't given him any chance to run away.

In the dime novels it's always dramatic, but in reality it's almost never dramatic. You just get it over with. He knew that, too.

"The key," I said.

"I'm sorry I killed your brother."

"The key."

It could have been a sob. I couldn't tell for sure. Maybe it was indigestion of some kind. It was just some kind of noise in him, some old-man noise maybe, coming out of him just ahead of the key coming out of his pocket.

He took the key out and said, "When?"

"I figure along about now."

"That's what I figure, too."

I shot him three times in the chest.

Chapter 23

The first train out arrived just before dawn. Jane waited on the platform with me. We'd had several cups of coffee and were edgy with it by the time the train pulled in.

"What will you do now?" she asked.

"Whatever they tell me to."

She smiled. "Still the good soldier."

"I suppose. I've been in harness so long I don't know what else to do."

She leaned over and kissed me on the cheek. "Thanks for listening to me go on so long about David this morning."

"What's six hours between friends?"

She laughed. "It probably seemed like six hours."

"The gun's safe. That's what matters." I said it sort of gruff. I wanted to say something to her—she was awfully damn pretty and almost frail there in her nurse's cape and cowl—but whatever came out would just embarrass me later when I thought about it. So I talked about work. Work talk is always something you can hide inside of. "I had it put in a special part of the storage car. I'll check it every stop or so."

Then the conductor was calling " 'board." He was silhouetted in the frosty dawn against a gold-streaked sky. The backyard roosters in town had started getting noisy.

"Take care of yourself," she said.

"You do the same, Jane."

You'd think that two grown-up people could think of something more original to say at times like these, but somehow we seldom do.

I squeezed her hand and then picked up my suitcase and walked to the train. When I got seated inside, we waved to each other and then the train lurched and started moving away from the platform. About thirty morning miles down the track I thought of a couple of things I should have said. But after sixty miles I was just as glad I hadn't said them.